J. Robertson

Poems Consisting of Tales, Fables, Epigrams, etc. etc.

J. Robertson

Poems Consisting of Tales, Fables, Epigrams, etc. etc.

ISBN/EAN: 9783744790093

Printed in Europe, USA, Canada, Australia, Japan

Cover: Foto ©Andreas Hilbeck / pixelio.de

More available books at **www.hansebooks.com**

POEMS,

CONSISTING OF

TALES, FABLES,

EPIGRAMS, &c. &c.

By NOBODY.

Procul efte Severi.

Keep your Diftance, Fellows, and I'll talk with you.

L O N D O N:

Printed for Meff. ROBINSON and ROBERTS, in
Pater-nofter Row; T. DAVIES, in Ruffel-
ftreet, Covent-Garden; and T. SLACK, in
Newcaftle.
MDCCLXX.

PREFACE.

HAVING *been some Months past out of Town, I called To-day at Mr Elzivir's, to know if my Poems were printed off:*—*He told me they were, and that he now waited for the Dedication; asking me at the same Time, who I designed that Honour for?*---" Dedication!" *says I*---" Why, suppose the Dedication was to " run thus"-----" *To* Every Body, *those Luminaries of Learning, those Patrons of Genius, those Candid Readers, those most Judicious Critics, &c. &c. &c.-----the Following* Farrago *is Dedicated by the humblest of their Admirers,* NOBODY." ————" Oh, dear Sir," *says* Elzivir, " that will never do: The Quibble " is stale: You might as well dedi- " cate it to your own Individual Self, " *(Nobody)* as to *Every Body:* Besides,

" that

" that Sneer upon *Every Body* wou'd fet
" *Every Body* a fneering at you ;---Con-
" fider, Sir, your very Name is a Bait for
" *Sarcaftical Quibbles.*—But what think
" you of chufing *Paoli* for your Patron :
" He's a glorious Subject for Panegy-
" ric, and his Name at the Beginning of
" your Book wou'd help the Sale greatly,
" efpecially if you were to have his Por-
" trait by Way of Frontifpiece *done* by
" an *Eminent* Hand :"—" Nèither will
" that do," *faid I*,—" Had it been an
" Epic Poem indeed, and the Hero of
" it fuch another as himfelf, I don't
" know how far my Vanity might have
" fpurred me ; but fhou'd I dedicate fuch
" a Trifle like this to him, the World
" wou'd be apt to think I was bribed by
" fome Great Man or other to throw an
" Affront on him." " I believe you are
" right," *replies* Elzivir, " and now I
" think again, I fear the poor Gentle-
" man ftands more in need to be Patro-
" nized than to Patronize :— Suppofe
" then," *added he*, " you dedicate it to
" the *Reviewers.*------" That," *fays I*,
" wou'd

" wou'd be vaftly impolitic, for as I am
" a Stranger to them, and intend to re-
" main fo, a hundred to one but in Re-
" turn for my Compliments they'd fall
" foul of me, as a Proof of their Im-
" partiality. No, no, hang it, I'll have no
" Dedication at all."—" You muft have
" a Preface, however," *cries* Elzivir :—
" That to me," *says I*, " feems as need-
" lefs as the other ; What can I fay in a
" Preface?—but that *' The following*
' Poems (or Small Talk in Rhyme, if
' you pleafe) were written at different
' Times and upon different Occafions, and
' not originally defigned for the Prefs:
' That they are now fent into the World in
' a loofe inconnected Manner :" " (for by
" the Bye, Mafter *Elzivir*, you have been
" rather carelefs in that Refpect, as you
" know that Part of the Affair was en-
" trufted to you)" " *That Avocations of*
" *a different Nature prevented the Au-*
" *thor's giving them a Revifal, (too much*
" *wanting, he fears): That the Oleo, fuch*
' as it is, is now offered to the Public with
' a hearty Welcome; and that Mr Cook

a 3   *' begs*

' *begs his Guests wou'd fall to, and eat*
' *heartily, or at leaft pick a Bit here and*
' *there, as the Dish is made up of various*
' *Ingredients, and none of them over large,*
' *or hard of Digeftion, he hopes:*"—" I can
", fay nothing but fuch Stuff as this ;—
" no, no, publifh it directly, and let the
" Brat take its Chance."——" My dear
" Sir," *replied* Elzivir, " a New Book
" without Preface or Dedication is as
" imperfect as a New Play without a Pro-
" logue : How can you think of thruft-
" ing yourfelf on the Public without a
" *By your Leave*, or *With your Leave:*—
" Or what wou'd you think, for Ex-
" ample, of a Stranger burfting into our
" Club-Room, and feating himfelf at the
" Table without a *Precurfor to announce*
" *his Approach*, or fome one of the Club
" to announce him?"—*I ftill perfifted in
my Refolutions of No Preface, not knowing, in fhort, what 'to fay upon the Occa-
fion, when Mrs Elzivir, who, I muft own,
has more Senfe than either her Good-Man
or myfelf, declared it her Opinion, That
a Preface would be neceffary, if it only an-*
fwered

swered the Purpose of adding three or four Pages to the Book; that it availed but little what was said in it, and that if her Advice might be taken, the Dialogue that had just passed between Mr Elzivir and me wou'd answer the Purpose as well as any Thing.

As I always pay an uncommon Deference to Mrs Elzivir's Opinion, I immediately took her Advice, and have, as near as I can recollect, verbatim, and without any additional Flourishes, scribbled down what was said upon the Occasion, which the Reader is entreated to look upon as a Preface; the common Intention of such Precursors (as my Letter'd Friend terms 'em) being generally to add a Something to the Size of the Book.

Jan. 11, 1770.

CONTENTS.

Aminter

The

ERRA-

ERRATA.

Page 3, after Line 8 insert the following Couplet, which was omitted,

> Met on the Downs in grave Debate,
> A *Patriot Shepherd* to create:

P. 4, L. 14, *for* Power,—*read* Pow'r.

P. 11, L. 9, *for* being—*r.* kindly.

Ditto, L. 15, *for* destroyed—*r.* destroy'd.

Ditto, L. 24, *r.* Which cut, again wou'd never shoot.

P. 15, L. 15, *for Sans* Trifling,—*r.* without it.

P. 41, L. 11, *for* Word,—*r.* Line.

P. 45, L. 15, *for* Mamma well knows,—*r.* Experience shows.

P. 46, L. 6, *for* drank,—*r.* drinks.

P. 50, L. 22, *for* under,—*r.* beneath.

P. 63, let the third Line run thus,

> Old *Charon* look'd confounded black.

P. 67, L. 11, *for* With Smiles they now appear,—*r.* they smiling now appear.

P. 100, L. 11, *for* gulph—*r.* gulp.

P. 149, after the 4th Line add the following Couplet,

> Whose Lives (their palsied Heads tho' grey)
> Are shorter than a Winter's Day.

P. 132, L. 12, *for* coward Tongue,—*r.* Magpye Tongue.

P. 183, L. 8, *for* Portals,—*r.* Portal.

The Reader is intreated to correct the above, and to excuse a few literal Errors and Inaccuracies, which have escaped thro' the Author's unavoidable Distance from the *Press.*

ORIGINAL POEMS.

The POET and STRAW.

A FABLE.

ON *Richmond* Hill with Doublet bare
 A hungry Poet takes the Air:
 The Air on *Richmond* Hill, tho' good,
 And excellent Camelion Food,
Is rather of too thin a Nature
For a beef-loving, two-legg'd Creature:
Our Poet stops, he looks around,
And murmurs thus in doleful Sound :

 " While Plenty o'er the Landscape reigns,
" Shall Bards alone feel meagre Pains?
" Ah, what avails, if in the Town
" My Madrigals acquir'd Renown ;
" If stranger to all-pow'rful Coin
" I seldom taste the rich Sirloin ;
" If for the Produce of my Brain,
" I meet from money'd Fools Disdain ;——
" In vain the Lawrel crowns my Brows ;
" What crowns my Pocket ?——Not one Souse :

A   " Of

" Of Bay or Lawrel, where the Use is ?
" Nor Bay or Lawrel Fruit produces :——
" I've Fame pursu'd, and now I've caught her,
" She proves——mere Moon-shine in the Water;
" How happier the unletter'd Glutton,
" Who can indulge on Beef and Mutton :——
" How curst each Servant of the Nine !
" I'd rather be a Fool and dine."

He said, and to his great Surprize
Beneath his Feet a Straw replies :——
" Ah, hapless Bard, look down and see
" Thy striking Emblem here in me ;
" Despis'd by those, to whom my Head
" Furnish'd the Staff of Living——Bread :
" That gain'd, behold me here cast down,
" Trod on by ev'ry sordid Clown :
" Just so the Bard, who from his Brain
" The hungry Mind can entertain,
" Is soon neglected and forgot,
" A barren Praise his hapless Lot ;
" To Fame becomes an empty Bubble,
" Trod on by Fools like Straw or Stubble."

The PATRIOT SHEPHERD.

A FABLE.

IN Days of Yore, when Beasts cou'd speak
  With the same Ease that Pigs now squeak,
A Flock of Sheep, high-wool'd, rich, free,
Enthusiasts to Liberty,
Who claim'd a Right, Time immemorial,
Like other Sheep-boroughs corporeal,
To chuse a Shepherd to attend 'em,
And eke from Injuries defend 'em ;
(The Sheep, in those Times, you're to note
Like Citizens cou'd give a Vote :)——
Among the Peasants who laid Claim,
To the Sheep-Guardian envied Name,
One Peasant far above the rest,
Was with the winning Virtues blest ;
For Liberty he bellow'd loud,
He tickled up the sheepish Crowd ;
Like them he talk'd, and always strove
By sheepish Tricks to shew his Love :
The Lady Sheep he oft carest,
To please the Ladies, laugh'd and drest ;
He flatter'd hard,——for Sheep, like Men,
Can swallow Flatt'ry——now and then ;
With them the Downs wou'd often strole,
Nibble the Grass, and drink the Pool ;

And

And more, to shew his gen'rous Mind,
His Gold was scatter'd like the Wind;
He brib'd so high, none dare oppose;
He soon was *chair'd*, and Shepherd chose.

Too true the Axiom we find,
Preferment warps the human Mind;
No longer now with Patriot Zeal
He ba'ad aloud for common Weal;
No longer nibbled on the Hill,
Nor longer, Sheep-like, drank the Rill :——
The Fish was caught, the Net thrown by,
Wove by that Demon, *Bribery*:
He talk'd of nothing but Obedience,
Of Shepherd's Power, and Sheep's Allegiance;
He fleec'd 'em without Rhyme or Reason,
Regardless of the Time or Season;
Drove them to Market, and there sold
His freeborn Sheep, for King-stamp'd Gold;
And when their Grievances they spoke,
He answer'd thus with sneering Look :

" Those Fools who sell themselves for Gain,
" Of Slav'ry never shou'd complain ;——
" And give me Leave, good Sheep, to tell ye,
" I bought ye, and by G——d I'll sell ye."

The Moral, Sir ?——I'm not inclin'd,
To hold a Mirror to the Blind.

MEASURE for MEASURE.

A TALE.

WITH Envy fraught and Malediction,
Fools rail againſt Church Juriſdiction;
They ſay, where Canon Law prevails,
That Juſtice never holds the Scales;
That in the civil Courts alone,
She and her genuine Train are known:
Falſhoods alike !——Where moſt ſhe's found,
The following Story may expound.

In old *Caſtile* ſome Ages ſince,
When fam'd *Alphonſo* rul'd as Prince;
A holy Prieſt, meek, chaſte, and good,
Happen'd to ſpill a Layman's Blood:
Ev'n Saints themſelves, in holy Writ,
Wou'd trifling Faults ſometimes commit;
No Rank the ſlaughter'd Fellow bore;——
A Reptile Shoemaker——no more:
By ſome malicious Folks 'twas ſaid
The Prieſt had grac'd *Criſpino's* Head;
And, taken in the Fact, had further,
To lewd Adultery added Murder;
Abſurd! to think a Churchman cou'd
In ſuch a Cauſe ſpill Chriſtian Blood:

When

When Priefts in thofe religious Times,
Were charg'd with any heinous Crimes,——
By Mother Church their Caufe was try'd;
Who elfe fhou'd Churchmen's Caufe decide?
And Juftice feated on Church-bench,
No doubt muft prove a fpotlefs Wench:
Thrice happy Age! When Canon Law
Unrival'd, kept the World in Awe:
But now, alas, the Cafe is alter'd,
And Priefts by Civil Law are halter'd;
Whence pious Churchmen now maintain
With Juftice——" this is *Satan*'s Reign."

By Virtue of Church Abfolution,
That wond'rous chymical Solution,
The Church has the exclufive Power,
Men's Souls from *Satan*'s Ruft to fcower;
To free 'em from corroding Sin,
And make 'em bright as new-made Pin:——
Shall thofe who by Cathedral Spell,
Can ope the Gates of Heav'n and Hell;
A Power to Kings as much fuperior,
As Earth to Heaven is inferior;
Shall thofe to whom fuch Power's affign'd,
No Defence from mere Mortals find?
Pay Churchmen little Veneration,
You fap the Church's beft Foundation;
And fhou'd the Church once tumble,——Hell
With Joy wou'd ring the World's laft Knell.

Am-

Ambaſſadors, ev'n at this Hour
Defy the Law's inferior Power;
Equally free to all Intent
With thoſe great Kings they repreſent;
And Prieſts from holy Writings ſhew
They're Heav'n's Ambaſſadors below;
(To puniſh any holy Prieſt
Is breach of Privilege at leaſt)
From whence this Inference they draw,
Prieſts are above the civil Law.

The holy Prieſt as Culprit ſtood,
Charg'd with the ſhedding Chriſtian Blood;
The Church ſat Judge, and Proofs came thick,
Inſpir'd no doubt by envious *Nick*;
The Priſoner *guilty* found;——and here,
Stop, Reader, and prepare the Tear;
That one in Rank ſo highly plac'd,
That one with *holy* Garments grac'd,
Shou'd for a trifling *Accident*
Meet ſo ſevere a Puniſhment:
But Mother Church has ſtill been known
Rather too rigid to her own;
A noble Leſſon to Mankind,
That Juſtice ever ſhou'd be blind:——
The Culprit firſt preſcrib'd Repentance,
The Court pronounc'd this dreadful Sentence.

" The

" The Fact fo plainly prov'd, the Church decrees,
" To terrify her Sons from Crimes like thefe,
" That from your holy Office as a Prieft,
" You be fufpended one whole Year at leaft."

Juftice thus fatisfied, 'twas thought,
The Affair wou'd fhortly be forgot;
But dire Revenge, conceal'd with Art,
Oft lurks within the Villain's Heart:
Crifpino's Son, for Mifchief rife,
Determines to have Life for Life:
Some Months *perdue*, like favage Beaft
(Vengeance ftill gnawing at his Breaft)
He waits——e'er Fortune brings his Prey
The harmlefs Prieft, within his Way;
When thro' his Heart, with Strength convey'd,
He drives the Dagger's murd'rous Blade;
The Prieft expires; the Murd'rer's feiz'd,
(Revenge thus got)——to die well pleas'd.

Can Crimes like this unmark'd pafs by?
No angry Token from the Sky?
No well-tim'd Earthquake to enclofe
(Churchmen all fav'd)——the Church's Foes?
No Thunder to proclaim to Earth,
That Priefts are of celeftial Birth?
But Heav'n-fent Miracles of late,
It feems are growing out of Date.

Tho'

Tho' Churchmen are in general tender,
They vow'd ftrict Juftice on the Offender;
To Court they fly, and quick *demand*
The Murd'rer yielded to their Hand;——
A Brother kill'd! Oh, impious Deed!
Ev'n Kings themfelves had better bleed;
They fix the Murd'rer's dreadful Doom,
Both here, and in the World to come.

His Majefty, quite cool and grave,
To their *Demand* this Anfwer gave.

" A Prieft a Layman kills :——The Caufe
" Was try'd by holy Churchmen's Laws;
" A Lay-man kills a Prieft :——This Time
" Our *civil* Law fhall judge the Crime."

The Hour will come, do all you can, Sir,
Satan fhall trim you for this Anfwer:

" Oh, *Becket! Dunftan! Hildebrand!*
" Ye Saints, whofe Names diftinguifh'd ftand,
" I'th' holy Calendar——look down——
" Avenge our Caufe—For 'tis your own."

The Trial comes ;——The Murd'rer caft,——
The King, as Judge, this Sentence paft:

" The

" The Fact fo plainly prov'd, the Law decrees,
" To terrify the World from Crimes like thefe,
" That for a Year the Privilege you lofe,
" Of making, or of mending Boots and Shoes."

How juft, how fevere was the Church's Decree!
How partial, how weak was the civil Law's Bann!
Look back thro' Time's Annals; in fhort, you
      may fee,
It has ever been fo, fince the World began.

The FEMALE CLAIM.*

A TALE.

LET Women their own Caufes plead,
    'Tis ten to one but they fucceed.

For many Years with conq'ring Sword
Tebald the brave, *Spoletto's* Lord,
His Valour 'gainft the Greeks had fhewn,
And fhook *Emanuel* on his Throne;
Yet tho' with Foes he ftrew'd the Plain,
His Hydra Foes ftart up again:
Surpriz'd, he found the more he flew,
His Enemies more numerous grew;

In

* The Story on which this is founded, is taken from the
ingenious Author of The Effay on the Writings, &c. of POPE.

In order to their Diminution,
He form'd the ftrangeft Refolution;
Throughout his Camp he Orders gave,
That ev'ry *Grecian* Captive Slave,
Who for the future fhould be taken,
Shou'd without Mercy be——*Caftraten*;
(A kind of Punifhment, ye Fair,
Poor *Abelard* was doom'd to bear)
And in that Order kindly fent
By Way of friendly Compliment,
To the *Greek* Emp'ror, in whofe Grace,
Caftratos held the foremoft Place;
For in his Court, as in our Nation,
Mufic was all the Hobby-Fafhion:
One Pipe deftroy'd, it was intended,
The other thereby fhould be mended:
For all your Naturalifts own,
That when the Bee becomes a Drone,
Tho', ftinglefs, he can work no more,
He *humms* far fweeter than before:
This *Tebald* boafted in his Mirth,
Was killing Foes before their Birth:
The Axe applying to a Root,
Which, if once cut, wou'd never fhoot:
" Oxen were harmlefs Beafts, he fwore,
" But Bulls enrag'd wou'd tofs and gore;
" And *Greeks* when of the *neutral* Kind,
" No Hydra Foes cou'd leave behind;

" Nor

" Nor with that holy Text comply,
" Which bids——*Encreafe and multiply.*"

Affairs for fome Time thus went on,
And many a Captive was *undone ;*
When - one Day *(Tebald* in his Tent,
Among his Lords in Merriment)
A *Grecian* Dame, whofe lufty Mate
Had by the cruel Hand of Fate,
Been Captive made, and bid prepare
To lofe——what Madam *cou'd not fpare,*
Into the General's Prefence broke,
And kneeling, thus the Prince befpoke :

" Is *Tebald's* Glory funk fo far,
" Againft weak Woman to make War ?
" And fhall that Sword, which in the Field,
" Has ever made his Rivals yield,
" Which not by Man can be withftood,
" Be poorly ftain'd with Woman's Blood ?——
" Heroes, and *Tebald* fure is one,
" To us have ftill Protection fhewn :
" A Cock counts all his Brethren Foes,
" But among Hens he peaceful crows ;
" Tho' Bull gores Bull, yet ftill he fcorns
" To plunge within the Cow his Horns :
" Have Mercy then, moft potent Lord,
" Nor with our Blood debafe your Sword."

The

The Prince, amaz'd, accofts the Dame——
" Why brand'ft thou undeferv'd my Name?
" When was it ever known, he faid,
" That Female Blood by me was fhed?
" Or fince the *Amazonian* Race,
" (Of your foft Sex the foul Difgrace)
" Can it with Juftice be averr'd,
" That War with Woman was declar'd?"

" What War more cruel, cries the Fair,
" Can *Tebald* 'gainft our Sex declare?
" You rob our Mates of what kind Heaven
" Has for our Health and Pleafure given;
" The joyous Fountain, from whofe Source,
" Pleafure pours with refiftlefs Force:
" It gives us in our Children, Wealth;
" Your Lady knows it caufes Health:
" To that, my Lord, each wedded Dame
" Pleads an *exclufive*, lawful Claim;
" And mutilating Nature's Stem,
" Is mutilating *Us*, not THEM:
" For Goods and Cattle I ne'er griev'd,
" Cattle and Goods may be retriev'd;
" But Woman,—once that Comfort gone,
" Is irretrievably undone:
" For Mercy then let Truth implore,
" Nor lay our Murders at your Door."

B

The

The admiring Chiefs with loud Applaufe,
Back her Requeft, and plead her Caufe;
Ev'n *Tebald's* Princefs, with each Look
A feeling Approbation fpoke;
For fhou'd the Chance of War, fhe thinks,
(And at the Thought fhe inward fhrinks)
Throw *Tebald* in the Captive's Place,
Alas! how frightful her own Cafe!——

  " Your Pray'r, quo' *Tebald*, fhou'd I grant,
" With All and every Thing you want;
" If on the hoftile bloody Plain,
" Once more your Hufband wear my Chain,
" Say Woman, what are you content,
" Shou'd be the Ingrate's Punifhment?"——

  " My Lord, the honeft Dame replies,
" My Hufband has——Legs, Arms, and Eyes;
" Thefe are his own;—and if once more
" Ungrateful, he fhou'd force your Power,
" They're yours, in Right of Victory;
" *Take them*, my Lord, but *rob not me.*"

  Tebald convinc'd, admits her Prayer,
No longer *mutilates the Fair*;
The army with a loud Acclaim,
Hail the plain-fpoken honeft Dame:——
The Chiefs with Prefents large reward her,
And thro' the Camp in Safety guard her:
                    Which

Which done;——with her beloved Spoufe,
She Arm in Arm jogs to her—Houfe;
Not quite recover'd of her Fright,
Till well *convinc'd*, that *All was Right*.

An EPISTLE *to a* FRIEND.

On T R I F L I N G.

FOR Want, Good Sir, of Something better,
I fend you here a Trifling Letter.

The Man who's fo amazing wife,
A little Trifling to defpife,
Tho' for a *Solomon* he pafs,
Is Trifle better than an Afs,
That on dry prickly Thiftles mumbles,
And cheerlefs ever, brays and grumbles:
Sans Trifling, Life were a poor Feaft,
Where Man would fit a Humdrum Gueft,
But Trifling, mirthful, full of Glee,
With Health to bear her Company,
Enters;—at once difpels our Gloom,
And kicks Spleen headlong from the Room.

Trifling to Wifdom's near ally'd,
Altho' by Pedants 'tis deny'd;
And in Truth's Maxims 'tis a Rule,
The graver, ftill the greater Fool:

Like

Like Mafter *Stephen*,* Sons of Folly
Are *greatly giv'n to Melancholy*.
And wife Men oft thro' Trifling's Road
Arrive at Wifdom's fnug Abode:
Aided by that, we Truths difcern,
·And Mankind's inmoft Paffions learn.

Cromwel, altho' he was no Fool,
Wou'd often romp like Boy at School;
And *Pruffia's* King fometimes defcends,
And blind-man-buffs it 'mong his Friends:
On Gravity when Monarchs trample,
Courtiers will follow their Example;
No longer then their Thoughts they ftifle,
Men's fouls are honeft when they trifle;
Hypocrify afide is thrown,
And for a Time Truth takes the Throne.

Scipio the Wife, in Days of Yore,
Oft trifled on *Cumea's* Shore;
With *Lelius* laugh'd, indulg'd his Freaks,
And play'd (Boy-like) at Ducks and Drakes:
And *Julius Cæfar*, as we read,
Was a true Buck of the firft Head;
And Bucks, I'm fure, muft be allow'd
To van it in the Trifling Crowd.

Ev'n

---

* A Charaƈter in *Every Man in his Humour.*

Ev'n *Solomon*, the Man moſt wiſe,
That ever breath'd beneath the Skies,
Had long thro' Pleaſure's Magic rov'd,
And all the Joys of Trifling prov'd:——
When he had got his *Quantum ſuff.*
Or rather more than was enough,
He *wiſely* ſaid—" That Life, alas!
" Was *Vanitatum Vanitas* :"
But when he conquer'd mawky Spleen,
He *wiſely* trifled on again;
And in old Age, as Records ſhew,
He kept a large *Seraglio*;
And all the Pleaſures he found there,
Were *Trifling*, we may ſafely ſwear.

May I aver, without Offence,
Trifling's a Thing of Conſequence?

Poets and grave Logicians own,
That all the World to Trifling's prone:
We ſee what Crouds diſpute and jar
On Politics, on Peace and War;
Or give a poſitive Deciſion
On *Patagonians*, or Religion;
On Inward Grace, or *Cock-lane* Ghoſt,
On *Nabobs*, or ſome favourite Toaſt;
On Op'ras; or on Matter's Eſſence,
On Farces, or the Soul's Quinteſſence;

On

On *Chatham*, *Bute*, or Patriot *Wilkes*,
On Cookery—or Price of Silks;
On Faith, that Anchor of Salvation,
Or fuch like Trifling Difputation;
What are they all but Trifling Jokes?
(At leaft made fo by Trifling Folks)
And yet thofe Trifles give Enjoyment,
By finding Trifling Minds Employment.

Your Graduates of *Grefham* College,
Maugre their Gravity and Knowledge,
Have lately to the World approv'd,
How very much they Trifling lov'd;
For Trifles they can fcold and prate,
And fight like Wives at Billinfgate:
Such Trifling we'd excufe—but when
They raife the death-denouncing Pen,
Pluck'd from the boding Raven's Wing,
It then becomes a ferious Thing;
" In pops grim Death, th' arrefting Serjeant,
" With—*Sir, your moft obedient Servant.*"

Ev'n at St *Stephen*'s fome Folk fay,
That Trifling bears a mighty Sway;
And yet I doubt the Truth,—for who
A Trifling Member ever knew?

Love by, Experience we find,
Chief Source of Pleafure to Mankind;

And

And Lovers' Actions always prove,
Trifling's the very Soul of Love.

Women are call'd in Ridicule,
The Trifling Sex by every Fool:
But Fools deſtroy their Spleen's Intent,
By paying them a Compliment:
What gains our Wonder and our Praiſe?
Their thouſand pretty trifling Ways:
By Trifling only they maintain
Their Empire, and deſpotic reign:
And Female Wit, which ſo ſurprizes,
From Trifling evermore ariſes.

But of all Triflers under Heaven,
Rhymeſters are moſt to Trifling given;
They ſpin in Trifles their poor Brains,
And get but Trifles for their Pains;
And what particularly ſhews 'em
Coxcombs, to every Soul that knows them,
Is,—That they boaſt with Fronts of Braſs,
Favours from Miſſes of *Parnaſſ.*
When ev'ry living Mortal knows,
Each Muſe is ſtill an unpluck'd Roſe.

Rhymeſters howe'er, may boaſt their Uſe;—
The Trifling Nothings they produce,
Serve Triflers on a rainy Day,
To *while* an idle Hour away.

Theſe

Thefe few, in fhort, may ferve as Samples,
Among ten thoufand like Examples,
That Trifling is a real Ingredient,
And to our Happinefs expedient.

But after all, Good Sir, I deem,
We fhould not, ufe it in Extreme :
Thinking and Trifling help each other,
As Friend helps Friend, or Brother Brother :⟶
Ev'n as the human Body tires,
And Sleep's recruiting Balm requires,
Trifling the fame Effect produces,
And fits the Soul for noblest Ufes:
In this the truest Wifdom lies,
Still to be Merry and be Wife.

Excufe, my Patron and my Friend,
Thofe trifling Cramboes which I fend ;
You're tir'd of Trifling by this Time,
And fo I'll end my Trifling Rhyme.

With Love to Friends, I'm your moft Fervent,
Obedient, Trifling, Humble Servant.

May *Four—The Day extremely fine* ;
Seventeen Hundred, Sixty-Nine.

PLUMB-

PLUMB-PUDDING.

A FABLE.

TWO Boys at Chriſtmas Dinner plac'd,
The Board a large Plumb-Pudding grac'd;
Their Plates well heap'd they glad ſurvey,
But each indulg'd a different Way:
Jack, who was greedy of the Plumbs,
Firſt pick'd them out, then lick'd his Thumbs;
He eat, and ſaid—" *'Twas ſpecial Good:*"
His Plumbs devour'd—The Remnant Food
Quite plain, now prov'd a worthleſs Store;
He taſted, but cou'd eat no more;
The Sweets had ſpoil'd his Reliſh quite,
Pudding unplumb'd gives no Delight;
And to acquire more Plumbs unable,
Hungry, he crying left the Table.

With much more Caution *Dick* proceeds,
And on the plumbleſs Portion feeds;
His Feaſt determin'd to conclude
With Plumbs, that rich, delicious Food;
But when the Plain was ſwallow'd, *Dick*
Had eat ſo much, he was quite ſick;
His Appetite, alas, was flown,
And ev'n for Plumbs his Reliſh gone:

Like

Like *Tantalus* he view'd his Store,—
And cry'd,—for he cou'd hold no more;
And what he'd fav'd with mifer Care,
A better Appetite muft heir.

He who his Plumbs unmix'd deftroys,
Will foon regret his fhort-liv'd Joys;
While He who keeps 'em for the laft,
Too late will mourn a blunted Tafte:
Then let us take the Plain with Sweet,
And like good Boys our Pudding eat,
Juft as 'tis cut us from above,
Nor Prodigals or Mifers prove.

✳✳✳✳✳✳✳✳✳✳✳✳✳✳✳✳✳

To a Difcarded FAVOURITE.

FLUTT'RING within a funny Ray,
A fhining Mote was heard to fay,
" In *Me* what Glories are difplay'd!
" For *Me* the Sun and Stars were made:
" For *Me*"——The Sun his Beams withdrew,
The *Mote* was loft——and fo are *You*.

FIDE-

F I D E L I A.

THE rolling Year, again brought on the Day,
 That fnatch'd from *Lucius* half his Soul away;
That Day on which he mournful Vigils kept,
And o'er *Fidelia's* Tomb in Anguifh wept:
Fidelia gone! Life is to him no more,
Than a lone Walk upon a dreary Shore.

 Deep Silence reign'd, the Midnight Hour was paft,
And Darknefs o'er the Globe her Veil had caft;
In vain the peaceful Bed invites to Reft,——
No Room for Peace in woe-fraught *Lucius'* Breaft:
Sigh follows Sigh, and Groan refponfes Groan;
Nor wonder, fince from Earth *Fidelia's* flown;
When fudden, quick as Light'ning, to his Sight
(Darknefs difpell'd) a Vifion heavenly bright
Stood at his Feet; the fmiling Form he knew,
And all *Fidelia* brightens to his View;
His Pulfes flutt'ring beat, he wou'd have fpoke,
But wild Amaze his half-form'd Accents choak;
When thus, in Sounds which long had blefs'd his Ear,
The Vifion ftrives her *Lucius* Breaft to cheer.

 " Can Sight of me, the lovely Phantom faid,
" (And fmiling fpoke) in *Lucius* raife a Dread?—
" With Smiles my *Lucius* erft was wont to greet,
" And his *Fidelia* ftill with Raptures meet;

" In

" In me the fame *Fidelia* you view,
" As loving, kind, as friendly, and as true.

 " That Hour, that long wifh'd Hour, which
    kindly gave,
" My Soul to Heaven, my Body to the Grave;
" To hear the Groans that rent your throbbing
    Breaft,
" While in your Arms my pulfelefs Corps you preft;
" While fix'd on me alone you groan'd Defpair,
" My pitying Soul ftill hover'd in the Air,
" Almoft reluctant flew to Joys above,
" For *Lucius* fhar'd with Heaven *Fidelia*'s Love.

 " Your Sighs, your Pray'rs, by me convey'd to
    Heav'n,
" Once more to Earth *Fidelia* have given;
" The heavenly Balm of lenient Hope to pour,
" And Peace, long banifh'd, to your Soul reftore:

 " Did Mortals know their Maker, they'd revere
" And glow with grateful Love, devoid of Fear;
" How merciful! How loving to Mankind!
" Their God! Creator! Parent and their Friend!—
" No Bug-bear Tyrant thirfting after Blood,
" But a kind Father, merciful and good.

 " How then can Man ungratefully prefume
" To paint th' Almighty with a Demon's Gloom?
" How can he impioufly a Tyrant call,
" That God who into Being *fmil'd* us all.
        " How

" How with a jaundic'd Eye to Heaven impart,
" A cheerlefs Picture from a cheerlefs Heart?
" Or with mean felfifh Views the World deceive,
" Or force with *Threats* their Vot'ries—to *believe.*

" When Death my *Lucius* from his Chains fhall
      free,
" And give him to immortal Joys and me;——
" (Oh, let not Death my *Lucius* affright,
" Death is our Angel-Guide to Realms of Light)
" With Love Seraphic fhall *Fidelia* tend,
" And lead to Raptures which fhall never end;
" Thro' Fields of Ether infinite to rove;
" New Scenes of ever-varying Blifs to prove:
" But what thofe Joys, or from what Fountains flow,
" Muft ne'er, fo Heav'n ordains, tranfpire below;—
" If known, Mortals wou'd burft their Chains of Clay,
" And rufh, unbidden, to the Realms of Day.

" Let *Lucius* then with Refignation wait,
" Till Death to Joys immortal fhall tranflate;
" And when Heav'n calls to a celeftial Birth,
" And bids releafe from Cares, from Pain and Earth,
" Boldly launch forth: Fear nothing; hope the beft;
" By me Heav'n thus commands,——*Hope, and be
      bleft."——*

She fmil'd, fhe wav'd her Hand, and fudden Night,
Conceal'd the lovely Image from his Sight:
Her Words to Peace his anxious Soul reftor'd,
And, kneeling, Heav'n with Gratitude he ftrait ador'd.

The PEDLAR and RASHER of BACON.

A TALE.

" WHAT on a Faſt-Day, thou vile Glutton!
" Thou Infidel! To feaſt on Mutton!——
" Nothing can fave you from the Birch,
" But Off'rings made to Mother Church;
" Elſe holy Candle, Book and Bell,
" Shall fign your *Mittimus* to Hell."——
Thus having threaten'd poor Lay Sinner,
Sir Prieſt fits down to a Fleſh Dinner;
And after ſhipping his own Cargo,
On others Guts lays ſtrict Embargo.

A Pedlar hungry, tir'd, and cold,
Who many a Mile that Day had ſtroll'd,
Came to a Peafant's friendly Hut,
Where he had often ſtuff'd his Gut;——
" How fare you, Pedlar?——Faith, fo, fo;
" I'm tir'd and hungry, you muſt know:
" Some good fat Collops I cou'd eat;"——
" Sure, quo' the Peafant, you forget:
" The Holy Church enjoins, to Day
" That we muſt faſt, confeſs and pray;"
(You're to obferve the Scene was *Spain*,
Where Prieſts and Saints defpotic reign)
" Two or three Onions are the Tote
" That journey'd this Day down my Throat;

" Nor

" Nor have I now one Morfel left,
" Of every Eatable bereft,
" But this fame Bacon Flitch, and fuch
" No Catholic wou'd dare to touch:"
The Pedlar caft a longing Eye,
He begg'd——he fwore moft bitterly,
" A favoury Rafher on the Coal,
" Was what he long'd for from his Soul;
" That Windows fhut, and Doors well barr'd
" 'Gainft Priefts and Saints wou'd fnugly guard;
" And after all, if he was caught,
" An Abfolution might be bought."

The tim'rous Peafant long deny'd,
At length thro' Pity he comply'd;
And having from the Pork-fide taken
A good large Sliver of fat Bacon,
" I wafh my Hands of all, he cries,
" At your own Door the Trefpafs lies;
" But if our Prieft fhou'd find you out,
" By th' Mafs he'll make a woundy Rout;
" Such Pennance he'll inflict——you'll wifh
" Your Bacon Slice had been a Fifh."

The Pedlar had his Rafher drefs'd,
His Looks a joyous Heart exprefs'd;
And to his Mouth without delaying,
The favoury Morfel quick conveying,
Juft at the Inftant, a loud Clap
Of Thunder——Lord have Mercy!——flap——

Came

Came like a bold intruding Gueſt,
To interrupt him in his Feaſt :
The Pedlar judging, that no doubt,
The Raſher caus'd this fearful Rout,
And that the Saints, with half an Eye
Had ſeen him ſmuggling from their Sky ;
The Morſel, Cauſe of all this Din,
Which Mouth had open'd to take in,
He drops amaz'd :——And with a Look,
Which Grief and Rage, and Hunger ſpoke ;
And daſhing down both Meat and Platter,
He cries——" Zoons, here's a Noiſe and Clatter
" About a footy Bacon Slice ;
" You Saints above are dev'liſh nice :——
" There,——now I hope you'll be quite eaſy,
" The Devil's in't, if this won't pleaſe ye ;
" Tho' by the Bye 'tis plaguy hard ;——
" You wou'd not like yourſelves to be thus ſerv'd."

(Tune, *Chevy-Chaſe.*)

Let Chriſtians hence on Faſt Days learn,
  Their Hunger's Tide to ſtem ;
For Saints, ſly Rogues ! can us diſcern
  When we ſee nought of them.

On Mrs. B—'s safe DELIVERY of a DAUGHTER, 1766.

AS *Jove* on high *Olymp.* was quaffing
   Nectar, and 'mong his Godlings laughing;
(For Gods and Godlings now and then
Can laugh and drink as well as Men.)
Petitions 'gainst the Trap-Door——thump——
As if from Cannon shot, came——plump;
And with such Force, that *Jove* amaz'd
Order'd the Trap-Door to be rais'd:*——
Which done;——without the least Decorum,
Prayers jostling Prayers, burst in before 'em;
And with such Noise,——*Jove* 'gan to stare,
And thought all *Billinsgate* was there;
For Mortals, in their Prayers, 'tis said,
Are often strangely underbred,
Nor to the Gods that Rev'rence shew,
That's due from clay-built Folks below.——
Some pray'd for Fame, and some for Health,
Some for a Wench——some pray'd for Wealth;
Thro' Fear of Hell some Wretches pray'd,
Some pray'd——for Praying was their Trade;
For Wives some pray'd——but well-a-day!
More pray'd——to take their Wives away;

Some

---

* See the Story of *Menippus* in the *Spectator*, No. 391.——In which, Prayers are said to enter Heaven thro' a Trap-Door, occasionally opened and shut as *Jupiter* happens to be in the Humour.

Some pray'd for this, and some for that,
And many for——they knew not what:
But what struck *Jove* more than the rest,
Were some short Pray'rs so warmly prest,
They spoke the Suppliants quite since e,
Which made *Jove* kindly lend an Ear;
For *Jove* (sly Rogue!) knows—from the Tongue
Or from the Heart, if Pray'rs are sprung.

" Great *Jove*, the Suppliants loud exclaim,
" Kindly assist the pregnant Dame,
" Guard *Bellamira* from Disaster,
" And safely guide——or, Miss or Master:
" No common Cause demands our Prayer,
" In *Bellamira* thousands spare.

This, and much more his Godship heard,
From many Suppliants preferr'd ;
But none more clam'rous seem'd than one,
An odd droll-looking Simpleton,
Who *Jove* in blundering Terms addrest ;
He own'd——This was his first Request,
And swore, if *Jove* wou'd kindly save her,
He ne'er wou'd ask another Favour.
Jove smil'd, and casting down an Eye,
Scrub on his Marrow-Bones did spy ;
Which plain as Sun at Noon-Day, spoke
The Affair to *Scrub* had been no Joke.

But

But what *Jove* thought was moſt obſervant,
Ev'n her own Spouſe in Pray'r was fervent;
For Huſbands ſeldom now a Day,
For their Wives Preſervation pray;———
He long to Peace had been a Stranger,
Joyleſs, his deareſt *Bell.* in Danger;
And wou'd have ſacrific'd his Life,
Unfaſhion'd Thing! to ſave his Wife.
Jove ſmil'd, and thought it ſomewhat ſtrange,
(For *Jove* himſelf is giv'n to Change)
That Mortals ſhou'd the Gods excel,
And from their Betters bear the Bell;
For be it ſpoken to *Jove*'s Shame,
Nor he, nor any of his Name,
To *Dinmow* Flitch cou'd e'er lay Claim.

To Conſtancy a perfect Stranger,
Jove in his Heart's an errant *Ranger*;
In ſnug Diſguiſe he often quits
Olymp. to feaſt on Mortal Bits;
And Fleſh and Blood prefers by th' Bye
To all the Beauties of the Sky;
For which Dame *Juno* ſcolds and hectors,
And pays him off with Curtain Lectures.

Yet *Jove* himſelf, tho' Buck compleat,
As e'er frequented *Ruſſel-ſtreet*,
To Mortals has forbad ſuch Jokes,
And threatens all your naughty Folks,

If they'll not mend and fay their Pray'rs,
Old *Nick* fhall carry 'em down Stairs.———
Hard Cafe! that *Jove* fhou'd Laws ordain,
Which *Jove* himfelf treats with Difdain:
But Laws were made to rule the Throng,
Your Gods and Kings are never wrong.

" My Friends, quo' *Jove*, ftroaking his Face,
" In Troth this is no common Cafe;
" Thoufands, you fee, in fad Contrition,
" For yon good Wife i'th' Straw petition;
" And *Viva Voce* all aver,
" Their Happinefs depends on her:
" The Knocker ty'd, the Straw thick fpread,
" The Nurfes hobbling round the Bed;
" The throbbing Breaft, the tearful Eye,
" Speak grim-fac'd Danger to be nigh:
" Then fly this Inftant;———downward fpeed,
" To aid her, in this Hour of Need;
" In *B———*'s Shape, *Lucina*, fhew
" All that *Obftetric* Art can do:
" You, *Phœbus*, quick to *Hull* repair,
" Affume your Brother *C———*'s Air,
" And Med'cine's utmoft Skill impart,
" To footh her Pains, and cheer her Heart:
" And, *Pallas*, fee your friendly Aid
" In *E———*'s lovely Form convey'd,
" That fav'rite Form you oft have wore,
" To charm the World with Wifdom's Lore;
" In

" In fweet Difcourfe *your* Med'cine pour'd,
" Will foften what *muft* be endur'd :——.
" While I, her lov'd Lord's tender Breaft,
" With Hope's fweet Balm will calm to Reft.

" And now, hear *Fate*——hear *Deftiny*;——
" By *Styx* I fwear :—'Tis *Jove's* Decree ;——
" Soon fhall a Cherub fee the Light,
" As *Venus* from the Ocean bright;
" And with a wonder-working Smile,
" Her fondling Mother's Pangs beguile :
" Her Welfare fhall be Heav'n's own Care,
" As Father wife, as Mother fair ;
" Like both in one, replete with Spirit,
" Good-nature, Wit——in fhort, all Merit.

" The Parents' Virtues to requite,
" Wing'd be their Days with true Delight;
" Health fhall her choiceft Bleffings fhed,
" The Loves fhall crown their genial Bed;
" Fortune with Smiles fhall ftill befriend 'em,
" And—Heaven's beft Gift—Content attend 'em;
" Bleffing and bleft, they long fhall fhew
" Example to Mankind below,
" That *Happinefs is Virtue's Prize*,
" And, *to be good, is to be wife.*

" And when Death fummons, as all muft,
" From whence they came, return to Duft,
" One

" One fingle Grave, one friendly Mold,
" In Union fhall their Clay enfold;
" Their Souls as one fhall ftill unite,
" And endlefs feaft in Realms of Light;
" On Earth their Virtues too furvive,
" And in their lovely Offspring live."———

Jove fpoke, and awful gave the Nod,
While *Fate* fubmiffive own'd the God.

The ROBIN's COMPLAINT to CLOE.

A SONG.

" WITHIN a wiry Prison bent,
"   Far from my constant Mate,
" O think,—with Pity think, dear Maid,
" How wretched is my Fate:
" Of me depriv'd, perhaps ev'n now,
" For Grief she yields her Breath;
" And Oh!--—I feel, depriv'd of her,
" I soon shall bow to Death.

" If in a Nunnery's gloomy Walls
" From Lovers' Joys debarr'd,
" Like me coop'd up---indeed you'd think,
" Your fate was wond'rous hard:
" Then as you wish yourself—to taste
" Love's Joys, and Liberty;
" Have Mercy on your little Bird,
" And kindly set me free."——

Thus in a narrow Cage confin'd,
 A *Robin* sweetly grieves;
Cloe relents;----and to her Bird
  Immediate Freedom gives:
The God of Love rewards the Fair,
  He fires her fav'rite Swain;
He gives her all Love's Bliss to know,
  Free from Love's bitter Pain.

The

The PEASANT and MASTIFF.

A FABLE.

WHERE *Nile*, the King of Floods, beſtows
His genial Bleſſings as he flows,
A widow'd Peaſant, that with Care
Foſter'd a darling Infant Heir,
The only Offspring of a Wife,
Dearer, when living, than his Life,
Abroad on urgent Buſ'neſs bent,
Forth from his homely Cottage went;
His Babe aſleep in Cradle lying,
(No further Need of lullabying)
His fav'rite Dog too left behind,
His Child and Houſe's Guard deſign'd:——
Ended his Buſ'neſs, ſoon the Swain
Returns to his lov'd Charge again;
He lifts the Latch, (his little Cot,
No other Bar or Fence had got)
His Dog with conſcious Sound and Tail
(In Dogs can Treachery prevail!)
Joy more than uſual expreſſes,
Twiſting his Form with fond Careſſes;
But, Oh, how great was his Surprize!
All ſmear'd with Blood the Dog he ſpies;
His frightful Jaws diſtain'd with Gore,
Suſpicious Marks of Murder bore:

The

The frighted Parent looks around,
No little Darling's to be found;
The Cradle overturn'd----The reſt
By Fear and wild Deſpair was gueſt;
The Infant's Fate each Object ſhews;
The Murd'rer in his Dog he views.
He rag'd, he tore his Hair, he ſwore,
And with a Hatchet which he bore,
Dealing a vengeful Blow, he ſtrait
Conſign'd the Maſtiff to his Fate;
Then headlong to the Cradle flies,
Which rais'd (Amazement all!) he ſpies
His ſmiling Treaſure on the Floor,
Aſleep, unwounded and ſecure;
And not far diſtant from the Child,
A monſt'rous Serpent, newly kill'd,
All torn and bloody, which 'twas plain
The faithful murder'd Dog had ſlain——
Slain in his Baby's dear Defence,
To ſave from Death its Innocence;
And in the Fray, ſo ſays the Fable,
Were overſet—both Child and Cradle.

If to the Moral you attend,
You'll ne'er unheard, condemn your Friend.

D

E D-

EDWARD *and* CLARA.*

"HASTE, *Edward,* hafte,---Oh, quick-
" ly hafte,
" Like Lightning fpeed away;
" And to where Love and Safety dwell,
" Thy *Clara* fwift convey.

" Nor darkfome Night, or Foreft drear,
" Can frightful Thoughts infpire;
" Since from a hated Lover freed,
" And an unfeeling Sire.

" The facred Rites, the fatal Pomp,
" Proclaim my deftin'd Doom;
" But fooner fhall To-morrow's Sun
" Behold me in my Tomb.

" Cou'd Parent fee his kneeling Child,
" And not incline an Ear?
" Not ev'n the Vulture will the Heart
" Of his own Offspring tear.

" What's

---

* *Clara,* Daughter of Earl *Witgulph,* being enamoured of *Edward,* a young Gentleman of inferior Rank and Fortune, made her Efcape into a neighbouring Foreft, (where fhe had appointed to meet *Edward*) in order to avoid a Marriage with *Edred* Earl of *Mercia,* to whom her Father had determined to *facrifice* her the next Day.

" What's *Mercia's* haughty Lord to me?
  " I fcorn a pageant Crown;
" While in my *Edward's* Heart I reign,
  " On Monarchs I look down.

" Have I a Parent loft?—My Friends,
  " My Kindred all unkind?
" Ah no!—all thefe, and much, much more,
  " In *Edward* I fhall find.

" What tho' I boaft a Thane my Sire,
  " Thou'rt not of low Degree:
" But what's compar'd to Worth like Thine,
  " A Tinfel Anceftry?

" Come, *Edward*, come; far from this Scene
  " Of Danger we'll remove;
" To ftay is Death: 'Tis *worfe* than Death,
  " Depriv'd of what we love.

" Hafte, *Edward* hafte---Thy *Clara* calls;
  " Oh, Whence this long Delay?
" Alas! I fear:—Thou wert not wont
  " Thus to prolong thy Stay."

She faid——And lo, a Voice was heard,
  Not Thunder more cou'd wound:
" O Heav'n!" fhe cry'd—For well fhe knew
  Her Father's awful Sound.

" Dege-

" Degenerate Wretch! Think not unknown
   " Thy purpos'd Scheme," he cry'd;
" Pursu'd, o'erta'en, thy low-born Choice,
   " Has for Presumption died—"

Her Eyes she rais'd:—Poor *Edward* lay,
   With many a Wound defac'd;
She scream'd—and falling on the Bier,
   His bleeding Corpse embrac'd.

No short-liv'd Eloquence of Tears
   Her inward Conflicts shew;
But in her Eye, all wild, appears
   Unutterable Woe.

" Unfeeling, barbarous, cruel Sire!
   " We never more will part:"
She drew a Bodkin from her Hair,
   She pierc'd her faithful Heart.

United now in one pure Stream,
   The crimson Channels flow;
And, as if conscious of their Fate,
   Blush with a richer glow.

An only Child destroy'd—The Thane
   Repentance feels too late;
And an unpity'd broken Heart,
   Soon gives him to his Fate.

Written

Written on a blank Leaf of SHAKESPEARE.

OH, *Shakespeare! Shakespeare!* How thy Magic
       charms!
Now wakes to Rage, and now as quick difarms;
Sooths, pierces, melts :—Hurries our Souls away,
Leaving untenanted our Shells of Clay.
Thofe Worlds which *Alexander* wifh'd in vain
With murd'ring lawlefs Conqueft to obtain,
Thy more victorious Pen (that Magic Wand!)
Charms from their Spheres to hail thy great Command:
Elves, Witches, Demons ftart up at thy Call;
You Naturalize, what *was* Unnatural.

   A fingle Word of thine delineates more
Than Pages from a modern Play-wright's Store:
Our Language is too weak to make thee known,
You form a richer Language of your own:
Shakefperian all!—You charm us, while around,
We tread *Parnaffian* confecrated Ground.

   In a fine Phrenzy rolling, your keen Eye
Pierces the Depth of vaft Profundity;
Quicker than *Jove*'s own Lightning rapid flies,
And at your plaftic Touch new Beings rife:
What Worlds are by thy wond'rous *Fiat* made!
Thou Great Creator! I had almoft faid.

The Critic's pigmy Bafis you defpife,
All Nature is the Bafe on which You rife;
To others as fuperior your Quill,
As *Atlas* to the Mole-conftructed Hill:
Like Larks at beft *They* fkim our nether Skies,
Whilft Eagle *Shakefpeare* to Heav'n's Summit flies,
Perches *Jove's* Sceptre, waits his awful Nod,
Or grafps the dreadful Thunder of the God.

If it be true what Critics oft have faid,
That Admiration is of Folly bied,
Grant Heav'n, that Folly's Paths I ftill attend,
And wear her Liv'ry to my Being's End.

The T O P S.

FROM School and from Grammar releas'd,
    as one Day,
Two Youngſters with Tops were indulging at Play,
With whipping and ſcourging while one was
    employ'd,
The other his Caſtle-Top coolly enjoy'd :—
Old *Lucius* their Tutor, who well knew the Art,
From Subjects moſt trifling wiſe Rules to impart,
Thus ſpoke as he ey'd 'em--"Good Pupils, obſerve,
" And cloſe in your Boſom this Leſſon preſerve:
" Young Boys are like Tops: Think a little,
    you'll find,
" Like Tops, that you're all of the verſatile Kind:
" Bad Lads are like Whipping Tops: From the
    Beginning,
" Quite idle, unleſs Signior *Whip* keeps 'em
    ſpinning :
" *E contra,* good Lads are like Caſtle-Tops found,
" Who ſpin free and willing without Laſh or Wound:
" A Laſh wou'd a Caſtle-Top's Spirits aboliſh,
" Would trip up its Heels, and its Spinning demoliſh;
" Good Boys too with whipping would ſoon loſe
    their Fire,
" While Idlers, like whipping Tops, laſhing require.
                 " Then

" Then wifely the Caftle-Top take for your
 Guide,

" Spin freely,——Scourge never fhall tickle your
 Hide."

On *our* MODERN COMEDIES.

SHakefpeare and *Johnfon*, with the learned Corps,
 Of Poets, much admir'd in Days of Yore,
From Nature drew their Characters like Fools;
Our modern Play-wrights follow wifer Rules:
Pictures from Life they fcorn to let you fee;
Not Nature—but what Nature *ought* to be;
Your low-liv'd Humor, Wit, and fuch poor Stuff,
In 'Times of Ignorance did well enough: ——
In this *Refin'd*, this Novel-reading Age,
They've banifh'd all fuch Nonfenfe from the Stage;
No Wonder Play-wrights fwarm in thofe bleft Days,
Sermons, they find, are eafier *made* than *Plays*.

Miſs NANCY.
A FABLE.

THE doating Parents grieve and fret,
  Leſt they ſhould loſe their only Pet;
Miſs *Nancy*, by devouring Sweets,
Was grown as pale as her own Sheets;
Have 'em ſhe wou'd—What Nurſe wou'd chuſe
So ſweet a Baby to refuſe?
For tho' a Prodigy of Wit,
Miſs had not ſeen four Twelvemonths yet;
To Death almoſt indulg'd, old *Mentor*,
Their grave Phyſician, quick was ſent for;
This Son of *Galen*, ſtraitway brib'd,
Bitters and Gruel were preſcrib'd;
But how, alas, ſhall Miſs be brought,
To ſwallow ſuch a nauſeous Draught;——
If Phyſic call'd, Mamma well knows
Miſs wou'd turn up her little Noſe.
Tho' very young, *Nancy* obſerv'd
Mamma with Tea was duly ſerv'd;
And oft ſhe whimp'ring cry'd—" 'Twas hard
" *Nancy* of Tea ſhou'd be debarr'd:"—
The Hint Mamma with Prudence takes,
In Tea-Pot the Preſcription makes,
The healthful Viand ſerves to *Nancy*;
This ſtraitway tickles Miſs's Fancy;
The Aparatus all declares
'Twas Tea on which Miſs *Nancy* fares;
                    And

And tho' her Face she sometimes screw'd,
" She vow'd her Tea was vastly good;"—
(Ev'n Nurslings strive with Might and Main,
For little Women to be ta'en)
And Milk, tho' sugar'd, henceforth scorning,
She drank her Med'cine-Tea each Morning;
Takes her disgustful Mess with Glee,
Because Mamma firnames it Tea.

Let not grown Wisdom with a Smile,
  Miss *Nancy*'s childish Folly blame;
For few now breathe in *Britain*'s Isle,
  But what are cheated with a Name.

On a beautiful Young LADY, *remarkably vain, who
died of the* SMALL-POX.

A Few Days fince *Cleora* fhone confeft,
 The lovelieft Nymph that ever grac'd
  our Plain,
And tho' by *Venus* and the Graces dreft,
 She was not half fo fair, as fhe was vain.

Admiring Swains fincereft Homage paid,
 New Conquefts ev'ry Hour her Charms could
  boaft;
But all thofe Conquefts which her Beauties made,
 Were by her boundlefs Pride and Folly loft.

How chang'd the Scene! No more fhe gives Delight,
 To foul *Variolæ** a lifelefs Prey;
Offenfive to the Touch, the Smell, the Sight;
 Who once admir'd—now loathing turn away.

That Form which moulded was from Beauty's
  Queen
 Raifes Difguft :—— Think, Virgins, think
  how foon,
Thofe Beauties now with Admiration feen
 May change, alas!—before yon weaning Moon.

       Beauty !

---

* The Small-Pox fo called.

Beauty! What is it but a fhort-liv'd Flower?
　　And what is Life itfelf? A Pigmy's Span:
Perhaps the Durance of a fingle Hour,
　　And Pride, curft Pride, was never made for Man.

On feeing a LAW BOOK bound in uncoloured Calf, and white Edges.

WITH unftain'd Edges, and in fpotlefs Calf,
　　A Law Book bound muft make a Stoic
　　　　laugh;
For in that ftriking Emblem you may fee,
Not what Law *is*, but what the Law *fhould* be:
A Law Book thus in the Law Livery dreft,
Is like a Jefuit in a Lay-man's Veft;
'Tis like a Strumpet cloath'd in fpotlefs White,
'Tis like a bitter Apple, fair to Sight;
'Tis like a fimple Quaker, plain and neat,
That with his Yeas and Noes is fure to cheat:
'Tis like a Pirate, that falfe Colours fhews,
Or *Hecla*'s Flames conceal'd in Virgin Snows;
'Tis like—In fhort, 'tis like Dan *Milton*'s Sin,
All fair without, but monft'rous foul within.

F E-

FEMALE CURIOSITY.

A TALE.

WHILE yet the World was in its Teens,
   (Of Centuries, the Poet means)
By *Jove* commiffion'd from above,
Straight to the Earth flew *Death* and *Love:*
As mutual Benefits defign'd
To fhed their Bleffings on Mankind.——
Love like a fair *Adonis* fhone,
Nor *Death* appear'd that Skeleton
Which modern Painters falfely fhew him,
(To judge from them you'd fcarcely know him)
His Face, tho' fomewhat pale and thin,
Was fmiling, and devoid of Grin;
He was, in Air, Shape, Voice, and Feature,
A decent, unforbidding Creature:
A Bow and Arrows either bore,
Both welcome Guefts at every Door;——
Death was commiffioned to fet free
Old palfied Age from Mifery;
And *Love* his Arrows to employ,
In dealing that inchanting Joy,
Without which Heav'n would tafelefs prove;——
For what were Heav'n, unblefs'd with Love?
Love's Pow'r the Young and Fair obey,
While Age hail'd *Death*'s obliging Sway;

Each courted as Man's guardian Friend,
Tho' widely different their End. ——

For fome Time Matters fmoothly went,
Happy the Young—the Old content:
When *Death* and *Love* travelling together,
The Ev'ning dark, ftormy the Weather,
Quick to a neighbouring Farm they fped,
They crav'd a Supper and a Bed:
The honeft Farmer and his Dame,
He *Camus* call'd,—*Demea* her Name,
With Hofpitality fincere,
A Welcome gave, and wholfome Cheer:——
The Guefts, to entertain the Peafant,
Crack'd Jokes, told Tales, and Stories pleafant;
Talk'd Scandal, and abus'd the Great,
Pity'd the Poor, reform'd the State;
They chatted, drank, and laugh'd, 'till tir'd,
Shook Hands, and then to Bed retir'd.

But our good Dame, who, by the bye,
Had fome fmall Curiofity,
Obferv'd the Quivers which each Gueft
With Care conceal'd under his Veft;
She wonder'd what they could contain,
She thought, re-thought—fhe rack'd her Brain;
And when her Guefts, all weary, flept,
She fnugly to their Chamber crept;
Their Quivers feiz'd, and ftrait withdrew,
Impatient the Contents to view;

She

She emptied 'em upon the Floor,
Eagerly view'd 'em o'er and o'er,
The variegated Feathers eyes
With Admiration and Surprize;
But fearing left her Guefts fhould wake,
And Umbrage at her Peeping take,
Hurrying—poor *Demea* fo commix'd 'em,
When in the Quivers fhe refix'd 'em,
That many of *Love*'s Darts convey'd,
Into *Death*'s fatal Quiver ftray'd;
And, *vice verfa, Death*'s were found
Among *Love*'s Arrows to abound;
Which prov'd the Source of fuch Miftakes,
Such unaccountable, ftrange Freaks,
That by this Accident fo fcurvy,
All Nature feem'd turn'd topfey turvey.—
Death's Arrows, twang'd from *Cupid*'s Bow,
Now breathlefs laid *Love*'s Votaries low;
And *Cupid*'s Darts, from *Death*'s fell Quiver,
Now for the firft Time pierc'd the Liver
Of ill-ftarr'd Age, who loud complains
Of Fires fhot thro' his fhrivell'd Veins:—
Hence we behold the wrinkled Dame,
With youthful Airs avow her Flame;
Or Square-Toes like a Coxcomb cry,
" If *Cloe* proves unkind, I die."---
In fhort, fince this curft blundering Æra,
Man's Happinefs is all Chimera.

Oh,

Oh, *Female Curiosity!*
Great Source of Man's Felicity!
How very much to thee we owe,
Let Mother, *Eve* and *Demea* ſhew:
What endleſs Bleſſings flow from thee,
Oh, *Female Curiosity!*

The UNFORTUNATE DAMSEL'S RESOLUTION.

An Old SONG, *newly written.*

NEar a Beckside, with Willow fring'd,
   The mournful *Dolly* lay;
And thus the Nymph was heard to sing,
   Or rather heard to say.

" 'Twas here, on this accursed Spot,
" That *Tummas* of the Mill,
" With Speechings fine first stole my Heart,
" And got his wicked Will.

" A thousand sugar'd Vows he swore,
" His *Dolly* he wou'd wed;
" Ah, *Tummas*, keep those Vows, or give
" Me back my Maiden-head.

" Upon this Willow will I hang,
" In pure Revenge and Spite;
" And if the Wretch dare lie alone,
" I'll haunt him ev'ry Night.

" I'll shake his Curtains—(but in Truth
" His Bed does Curtains lack)
" And plague him, till the Morning Cock
" Obliges me to pack.

" Or thro' the Church-yard shou'd he go
" By Night—my Ghost shall rise,

                                    " And

" And like a *headlefs* Horfe appear,
  " With *frightful Saucer Eyes:*

" No Fear the perjur'd Man can hire
  " (Too great will be the Coft)
" Our Book-learn'd Prieft, in the *Red Sea,*
  " To lay my troubled Ghoft.——

" Upon this Willow will I hang,
  " Ev'n here beneath this Tree ;"——
She faid——and flipt her Garters twain
  From juft above her Knee.

The fatal Noofe poor *Doll* prepares,
  Her Lover fprings the Beck ;
" Ah, *Tummas,* art thou there," fhe cries,
  And hangs——*upon his Neck.*

From this Example learn ye Swains,
  Nor henceforth perjur'd prove,
For Girls *undone,* are apt you fee,
  To hang themfelves for Love.

The FISHERMAN.

A FABLE.

UNknowing and unknown to Fame,
   An honeſt Clown——*Dorus* his Name,
With fraudful Line, and baited Hook,
Near the Sea Shore his Station took,
In hopes the Cravings to ſupply
Of a large helpleſs Family:
But Fortune, who her Favour ſheds
Seldom upon deſerving Heads,
On *Dorus* glanc'd with ſcornful Spite;
No Prize——not ev'n a ſingle Bite.
Tir'd with ill Luck he now deſpairs,
And for a hungry Home prepares;
When to his Joy and great Surprize,
He feels a Fiſh of monſtrous Size,
(So flatters ſmiling Hope)——When, lo——
Fortune again appears his Foe;
He drags on Shore, with cautious Pull,——
A Fiſh?——Ah no——a Human Skull;
A ghaſtly and forbidding Treat,
Improper Food for him to eat:
What can he do?—Shall he again
Commit his Capture to the Main?
But here Humanity prevails,
And Piety his Heart aſſails:

                              " Who

" Who knows, cries *Dorus*, with a Sigh,
(A Heart-fprung Tear in either Eye)
" But this might once a Portion be,
" Of a poor Spoufe, or Sire like me;
" On whofe Endeavours a large Brood
" Of Little Ones might hang for Food;
" Shipwreck'd perhaps in Sight of Land,
" Or murder'd by fome Villain's Hand;
" My Duty and my Feelings too
" Strongly evince what I fhou'd do;
" The Kindnefs which to him I fhew,
" Perhaps to others I may owe."

So faid, away the Skull he bears,
And in the Woods a Grave prepares :
He digs——his Heart dilates with Pleafure
To find a Heav'n-fent golden Treafure ;——
A Treafure to his utmoft Wifhes,
Superior to ten thoufand Fifhes;
With which he joyous marches Home,
The Skull bequeathing in its Room.

Thofe Hearts that with Humanity diftend,
In Providence are fure to meet a Friend ;
And the fame Love we to our Brethren fhew,
Our Heavenly Father will on us beftow.

⁂

The CONFESSORS.

WIth Creſt commanding, and Cathedral Look,
   Thus to *Alvarez* Father *Gerald* ſpoke:
 " Regardleſs of your Soul, whence comes it, Son,
 " Day after Day, that thus you Shriving ſhun?
 " Thoſe who with Mother Church run high in Tick,
 " Will find their Priſon Hell, their Jailor *Nick:*
 " Learn from your Wife, nor longer go aſtray,
 " She, pious Soul, ſhrives almoſt every Day."
Alvarez, who oft thought in jealous Mood,
That Madam's Shriving boded him no Good,
Yet durſt not to Sir Prieſt behave uncivil,
For Fear of Inquiſition and the Devil,
Thus made Reply:——" Our virtuous Wives,
       Heav'n bleſs 'em!
 " Have handſome well-fed Fathers to confeſs 'em;
 " Had we to ſhrive Us, Females young and gay,
 " We ſhou'd at leaſt be as devout as they;
 " Upon our Knees we oft ſhou'd fall before 'em,
 " Diſſolve in Bliſs, and perfectly adore 'em."

Alvarez judg'd wiſely:——Were Nuns made
     Confeſſors,
T'inflict proper Penance on *bearded* Tranſgreſſors;
As Father Confeſſors to Females are tender,
So Lady Confeſſors wou'd prove to our Gender;
Ev'n *Whitfield* and *Weſley* wou'd Converts become,
And all the World own the Religion of *Rome.*

The SWINE and ERMINE.

A FABLE.

THou filthy Beaſt, thou worſe than Vermine
   (Thus to a Swine exclaims an Ermine)
Avaunt——at proper Diſtance know
The Diff'rence 'twixt a Clown and Beau :
A Swine! There is not in all Nature.
So dirty, underbred a Creature :
How can Mankind ſuch Neighbours bear ?
You poiſon and pollute the Air.

   Thou gawdy *Nothing*——with Diſdain.
Retorts the Swine, thy Pride refrain ;
Such Finnikin ſpruce Things as you
With juſt Contempt and Scorn I view :
Let Man our different Worth decide,
His Judgment ſoon ſhall quell your Pride ;
We and our numerous taſteful Breed,
Thouſands and thouſands daily feed :
From Putrefaction muſt ariſe
Steams fraught with Death, which otherwiſe
By Man imbib'd, with earlieſt Breath
Wou'd ſweep the Human Race to Death ;
By us this Putrefaction taken
As Food, becomes good Pork and Bacon ;
Concocted thro' our Chymic Veins,
It yields both wholſome Food and Gains ;

                     And

And ev'ry Swine may boaſt, good Sir,
That he is Nature's Scavinger:
Ev'n you yourſelves, in a great Meaſure,
Our Debtors are for Health and Pleaſure:
The holy Prieſt will take our Part,
Sir *Hugh* loves Tythe Pig from his Heart;——
Riches we give and Suſtenance,
While all your boaſted Excellence
Is——with that worthleſs Skin of thine,
To make your Brother Coxcombs ſhine.

Judge not of Worth by ſplendid Shew,
A Clown's more uſeful than a Beau.

A L E X·

ALEXANDER *the* GREAT.

AS *Alexander*, (all the World ſubdu'd)
 Amid a Throng of circling Courtiers ſtood,
" In Me, he cry'd, Great *Ammon*'s Offspring view,
" To mighty *Jove* my Origin is due ;
" Let favour'd Monarchs ſwell young *Ammon*'s
   Train,
" My Father's Viceroy, God-like, here I reign ;
" Whate'er I will's the Will of mighty *Jove* ;
" On Earth I rule, as he commands above."
He ſpoke :——Adoring Courtiers proſtrate lay,
When a poor *Crow*, whom Chance had brought
    that Way,
As high in Air, he o'er the Monarch ſped,
Croak'd loud Diſdain, and *ſh——t* upon his Head.

A New HYMN *by a* PREACHER *of* THE WORD, *in Imitation of the Inimitable* Moravian *and* Methodiſtical *Hymns.*

THY Faith, O Lord, in Bleſſings ſhower,
    That Sinners may thy Saints believe;
For were it not for Faith's ſtrong Power,
    In faith thy Servants cou'd not live.

Careleſs of all that *Satan* can,
    Armies of Fiends we will not fear,
While General *W———d* leads the Van,
    And General *W———y* guards our Rear.

And for theſe Sinners who dare go
    To ſee a Play,——their Eyes put out;
And at Aſſemblies, Mercy ſhow,
    In giving all who dance——the *Gout.*

As *Forte* let our Groans be ſtrong,
    Our Sighs *Piano*——diſmal——ſad;
Allegro is the Devil's Song;
    True Saints *ſhou'd* mourn,——Fiends *will* be glad.

Yet may each Brother in the Faith
    A Dove-like gentle Siſter find,
To ſport with him in Love's ſweet Path,
    And friſk and bound like wanton *Hind.*

F   Our

Our Lives in Love thus may we ſpend,
  And love and friſk, and friſk and love;
And when our Love on Earth we end,
  Grant we may friſk and bound above.

Full well we know that *Sion*'s Keys,
  The Keys of *Sion*'s Mount are given
To us——to let in whom we pleaſe,
  Thro' the *ſtrait* Turnpike Gate of Heaven:

Where faithful Travellers of Courſe
  Muſt pay the Turnpike as they paſs;
A good round Sum for ev'ry Horſe,
  But a far rounder for each Aſs.

The TWO KINGS.

A FABLE.

CRoſſing the River *Styx*, with Shoals
Of new departed motley Souls,
Old Skipper *Charon* look'd damn'd black,
Leſt with the Load his Boat ſhou'd crack;
Tho' Souls, as Souls, are lightſome Freight,
Their Sins oft prove a deadly Weight,
And ſhou'd their floating Carriage fail 'em,
Not ev'n Cork Jackets wou'd avail 'em:
His Boat chuck-full,——ſuch ſcreaming roſe
From Nurſes, Miſſes, Ladies, Beaus,
That *Charon* rais'd his Voice and ſwore,
While Echo anſwer'd from the Shore,
" If they continu'd their damn'd Tricks,
" He'd ſouſe 'em every one in *Styx*,"
And aſk'd 'em with a Phiz moſt grim,
If they had ever learnt to ſwim:——
In ſhort he ſoon becalm'd the Riot,
And made 'em tolerably quiet:
He trim'd his Boat, and with a Frown,
Damn'd 'em, and made 'em all ſit down.

Order obſerv'd in ſome Degree,
A Ghoſt of high Pompoſity,
With courtly Air and ſcornful Look
Thus to his Brother Shadows ſpoke:——

" Hence,

" Hence, Reptiles, hence—your Diſtance know—
" Due. Homage to a Monarch ſhow;
" Shall one of my illuſtrious Birth,
" A King,——a Deity on Earth,
" Be crowded thus with the *Canaille*,
" Fellows who ſtink of Beef and Ale?
" You, *Charon*, with that dirty Face,
" Depend on't, you ſhall loſe your Place;
" My Brother Sovereign *Pluto* ſoon
" Shall make you ſmart for what you've done:
" Reptiles, avaunt——at Diſtance tend;
" Your Touch, Looks, Manners, all offend."

Old *Charon* grumbling in his Maw,
Damn'd him, and bid him *hold his Jaw*;——
Whilſt One, who living,——from the Stage
Had often entertain'd the Age,
With Whim *Cervantic* in his Face,
Firſt bowing, thus addreſs'd his Grace:——
" All Hail—Great King, Great Monarch, Hail!
" Frown not, I'm not of the *Canaille*;
" In me your Brother *Brentford* view,
" I've been a King as well as you;
" Like you have worn a Pageant Crown,
" And aw'd the Millions with a Frown;
" Like you too, Brother *Phiz.* reſign'd,
" And left my Pageant Crown behind:——
" But now——Good Sir, be not offended——
" The Curtain dropt, the Farce is ended:
" Tho

" Tho' Fortune for the Stage equipt us,
" Our Wardrobe-keeper, Death, has ſtript us,
" And the rich Robes on Earth poſſeſt,
" Lie folded in the Grave at reſt :——
" Maugre the Rank we living bore,
" Like theſe we're Shadows now——no more;
" All, Brothers All——at leaſt in this,
" We're but *Perſonæ Dramatis*;
" Like them we're bound to Critic Hall,
" By Critic Rules to riſe or fall;
" Where Kings, Lords, Beggars, all muſt ſtand,
" And undiſtinguiſh'd hold the Hand,
" While Critic *Minos* and his Jury
" ('Tis true, good Brother, I aſſure ye)
" Will hiſs or clap, juſt as they find
" We've play'd the Characters aſſign'd;
" Where Birth and Rank paſs unregarded,
" And Merit only is rewarded."

He ſpoke——the Monarch ſighing, ſwore,
" He never heard ſuch Truths before."

EPI-

EPIGRAM.

FOur Hours *Volusius* spent the other Day,
  With three grave learned Fellows of our
    College,
And when he left 'em, thus was heard to say,
" Oh, the amazing *Ignorance* of *Knowledge.*"

EPIGRAM.

WIthin a Bracelet's Circle *Will* appears,
  Which on her Arm his loving Spousy
    wears ;
Will in Return his *Sophy's* Portrait shews
Dependant from his Watch where'er he goes ;
With equal Truth their Passion they impart,
Both Arm and Fob are *distant* from the *Heart.*

HENRY

HENRY and SOPHY.*

I.

HENRY and Fortune now are Friends,
  His many Sorrows all are paft;
Fortune to make him full Amends,
  Gives to his wifhing Arms at laft.

II.

The long-lov'd *Sophy*; faireft Maid
  That ever caus'd or felt Love's Smart,
In her moft richly were difplay'd
  The lovelieft Form and trueft Heart.

III.

Long had their Friends with Souls fevere
  Oppos'd the Lovers happy Fate;
But chang'd——with Smiles they now appear,
  And *with* 'em at the Altar wait.

IV.

The Holy Prieft pronounc'd aloud
  The *Gordian* Wonder-working Spell;
While *Love* and *Hymen* both avow'd,
  " Shrin'd in their Breafts they'd ever dwell."

" And

* This and the following are founded on Facts,

V.

"And art thou mine," the Bridegroom cry'd,
 "With all thy wond'rous Truth and Charms?"
She fmil'd—fhe wou'd have fpoke—fhe figh'd—
And ftraight expir'd within his Arms.———

VI.

Too weak to bear Joy's rufhing Flow;
 Her tender Frame refigns her Breath;
This Moment in Love's Arms——and now,
 Enfolded in the Arms of Death.

VII.

In vain, in vain you fly for Aid;
 Life fhall no more that Form relume;
The Marriage Bed, ill-fated Maid,
 For thee ordain'd, is a cold Tomb.

VIII.

While Floods of Tears and piteous Moan,
 A genuine Sorrow teftify;
Silent poor *Henry's* feen alone,
 No Tear bedews poor *Henry's* Eye.

IX.

Homeward his *Sophy's* Corpfe he tends,
 Frantic his *Sophy* he enfolds;
That friendly Night his Sorrow ends;
 One Grave the New-wed Lovers holds.

We

X.

We graſp at Joys within our Reach;
  We graſp, and catch a wat'ry Bow:
Leſſons like theſe ſhou'd Mortals teach,
  True Joy exiſts not here below.

AMINTOR

AMINTOR and ANNA.

I.

CURST with a conscious feeling Mind,
  The poor *Amintor* lay,
Within a cheerless Jail confin'd,
  And sigh'd his Hours away.

II.

To save a Friend of Means bereft,
  Amintor enter'd Bail;
Friends oft prove false——*Amintor*'s left
  To languish in a Jail.

III.

Where are those Friends, *Amintor*, where
  Your Summer Days cou'd boast?
Like Insects now they disappear,
  Kill'd by a wint'ry Frost.

IV.

No Friend, save One, now anxious came
  To heal Misfortune's Wound:
That Friend, true to his Peace and Fame,
  Was in his *Anna* found.

Hymen

V.

Hymen and *Cupid* wove the Chain,
 That link'd her to his Heart;
With her he half forgot his Pain,
 Nor felt Affliction's Dart.

VI.

Tho' all the Charms that Beauty knows,
 Were in her Form expreſt,
Yet faint her outward Charms, to thoſe
 That lodg'd within her Breaſt.

VII.

A thouſand namelefs Arts ſhe try'd
 To ſooth his anxious Mind:
" My Dear *Amintor*, oft ſhe cry'd,
 " Heav'n will at laſt prove kind.

VIII.

" Affliction's Cloud once overblown,
 " Joy, doubly Joy appears;
" The Morn o'ercaſt, the Noon-tide Sun
 " A ſtronger Brightneſs wears.

IX.

" Virtue eſſay'd ſtill mounts the higher,
 " And nobler Worth aſſumes;
" As Gold, when Droſs-rid by the Fire,
 " More pure and rich becomes.

" While

X.

" While Innocence and Goodnefs reign
 " In my *Amintor*'s Breaft,
" Our Fate with Courage we'll fuftain,
 " And leave to Heav'n the reft."

XI.

Chearful *with* him, fhe ftill appears
 The Meffenger of Hope ;——
When *from* him,——to her fmother'd Tears,
 She gives a boundlefs Scope.

XII.

The Rofe, that erft with blooming Grace
 Had with the Lilly fhone,
By Grief was wither'd :——In her Face
 The Lilly reign'd alone.

XIII.

Soon as the Lark falutes the Day,
 Each Morning *Anna* flies,
To chafe corroding Spleen away,
 And blefs *Amintor*'s Eyes.

XIV.

A long, long Day——No *Anna*'s feen ;——
 Her Abfence caufes Dread ;——
When filent, Grief cuts far more keen,——
 She preffes a fick Bed.

       " The

XV.

The News when brought, he raving cries,
  " Oh Wretch accurſt !——For Thee,
" For thee the Faithful *Anna* dies,
  " Her fated End I ſee.

XVI.

" 'Tis thy accurſed Hand that throws
  " The deadly murd'rous Dart,
" 'Tis Thou art Author of her Woes;
  " Thou, Thou haſt broke her Heart.——

XVII.

" Thy *Anna* and thy little Son
  " To thee their Ruin owe;
" Thy fatal Folly has undone,
  " All that is good below."——

XVIII.

No more, *Amintor*, now complain,
  Thy *Anna*'s amply bleſt;
Of Fortune and her glitt'ring Train,
  To utmoſt Wiſh poſſeſt.

XIX.

A Kinſman Carle, whoſe griping Hand,
  When living was unkind,
Dying, bequeath'd her all his Land,
  Sore griev'd 'twas left behind.

      The

XX.

The News to *Anna* Health imparts,
 Joy ſparkles in her Eyes;
From her forſaken Couch ſhe ſtarts,
 " Thanks! gracious Heav'n!" ſhe crie .

XXI.

" Is *Anna* then ordain'd to give
 " *Amintor* Liberty?
" For his lov'd Sake I wiſh to live,
 " For him well pleas'd wou'd die.

XXII.

" For him and my poor Babe——Oh, grant,
 " This Flood of Joy I bear;
" Kind Heav'n has given me all I want,——
 " Henceforth *I'll not deſpair.*"

XXIII.

To Providence the grateful Tear,
 Burſts from her up-rais'd Eyes;
Not Hecatombs to Heav'n appear
 Such pleaſing Sacrifice.

XXIV.

With Tranſport fir'd, ſhe eager ran,
 To make *Amintor* bleſt:
She ſaw *Amintor*——ghaſtly,——wan——
 In ſhrowded Garment dreſt.

Frantic

XXV.

Frantic that Morn he rav'd——" I ne'er
" Shall *Anna* fee again ;".
He falls a Prey to black Defpair;
   His Heart-ftrings burft in twain.

XXVI,

The Weaknefs which from Virtue grows,
   Can Juftice faulty deem ?——
Such Weaknefs Virtue only knows,
   When *Virtue's in Extreme.*

XXVII.

Let callous Bofoms moralize,
   And frigid Rules lay down;
They feel not who are over-wife,
   Or dart the *Stoic* Frown.

XXVIII.

Like *Niobe* a while fhe ftands,
   Then finks upon the Floor,
She lifts her Eyes——She wrings her Hands,
   And never rifes more.————

XXIX.

One fuch Example here below,
   (In Heav'n let Virtue truft)
Does an hereafter plainly fhow;
   God cannot be unjuft.

An ENCOMIUM.

I.

MORTAL was never yet fo grac'd,
   With partial Bleffings from the Skies,
As *Draco*;—Rich in every Tafte
That Men of real Worth—*Defpife*.

II.

A Youth more lovely, more polite,
   More witty, graceful, more refin'd,
Or one more form'd to give Delight,
   Was never feen—*In his own Mind*.

III.

" *Study thyfelf*,"---(Thus Sages write)
   " In Wifdom's Lore if you'd furpafs:"
Draco each Morning, Noon, and Night,
   Studies Himfelf—*Within the Glafs*.

IV.

His Learning, his amazing Knowledge,
   Impartial Judges muft confefs,
Unequall'd ev'n by Heads of College,
   In that moft noble Science—*Drefs*.

Some

V.

Some filly Folk who know him not,
　Aver, he's got an empty Skull;
Can Emptiness then be the Lot
　Of one who—*Of himself's brimful.*

VI.

His Tongue such Torrents does difpenfe
　Of Words;—we're ftruck with wild Amaze;
Thefe Torrents ne'er can give Offence,
　Tho' much he talks—*He Nothing fays.*

VII.

To Truth fo very warm a Friend,
　Mortal by him was ne'er deceiv'd;
In this he never can offend,
　For *Draco—never was believ'd.*

VIII.

His Courage in the open Field,
　Was never doubted Day or Night;
Nor was he ever known to yield,
　For 'tis well known—*He dares not fight.*

IX.

Whene'er the lovely Swain draws near,
　The Ladies all around him flock;
At Sight of him they glad appear,
　For he's their favourite—*Laughing Stock.*

X.

So very amorous the Youth,
  Still making Love, ſtill ogling, ſighing,
Obſerve him, and you'd ſwear, in ſooth,
  He cannot live—*unleſs he's dying.*

XI.

But ſhould a Fair One equal die,
  And Face to Face our Youth aſſail;
Gods! with what Eagerneſs he'd fly—
  Backwards,—*like Cur with ſhrunk-in Tail.*

XII.

Proceed, dear Youth—Dear Youth, proceed,
  To other Youths Example ſhow;
And let 'em in your Actions read,
  Not what they *ſhou'd;* but ſhou'd *not* do.

St C A-

St CATHERINE.

A FABLE.

A Reverend Monk and honest Clown
Journey'd towards a Market Town;
The Time. beguiling as they walk,
Like other Trav'llers, in small Talk;
'Till Chance directed to a Road
Where good St *Catherine*'s Image stood;—
The pious Monk Obeisance made,
Th' unheeding Clown nor bow'd or pray'd,
But onward pass'd :----Struck with Surprize,
" What are you blind?" the Father cries;
" Behold where good. St *Catherine* stands;
" The Saint your Reverence demands:
" Quick on your Knees Atonement make,
" Lest Heav'n's high Wrath in Thunder break
" O'er your devoted Head:"—The Clown
Regardless of the Father's Frown,
Laughing reply'd;—" What there you view,
" Within my Orchard lately grew;
" And that fine Form which now it shews,
" To *Mudge* the Carpenter it owes.
" Shall I in Reverence bend the Knee,
" To an old Stunt Crab-Apple Tree?
" If that grim Lady is a Saint,
" (That Piece of Wood bedaub'd with Paint)
                              " My

" My Orchard muſt be *Holy Ground,*
" Where holy Apple Trees abound."

" A Tree I own it *was;*—or rather
" A downright Log," replies the Father;
" 'Till Church by holy Ordination,
" (A Kind of Tranſubſtantiation)
" Has giv'n the Log a new Creation.
" A Saint *'tis now* in every Senſe,
" Therefore atone for your Offence;
" Beg good St *Catherine's* Interceſſion,
" To cleanſe you from your foul Tranſgreſſion;
" Or *Satan* with his Brimſtone Pickle,
" Your carbonaded Hide will tickle."---

The frighted Peaſant knelt and pray'd,
Then riſing—ſhrugg'd—and ſighing ſaid;
" That ſhe's a Saint I'll not diſpute;
" The Church commands—and I am mute;—
" And yet—Shall I my Weakneſs own?
" To me ſhe ſeems a *Wooden* one;
" Ev'n at the Inſtant I adore,
" I can't help thinking of the *Crabs* ſhe bore."

How many titled *Things* we find,
Set up as Idols for Mankind!
Who, when their Worth intrinſic's underſtood,
Are meer St CATHERINE's—*gilded Sticks of Wood.*

The

The PUPPET-SHOW.

A TALE.*

AT *Skipton* Wake, where once a Year,
With Sports and Paftime and good Cheer,
The Lads and Laffes blythe regale,
And feaft on Cheefe-cakes, Tarts, and Ale;
(Wakes! the old Midwive's conftant Friend,
Where frolic Love and Joys attend;
Where mad-cap Pranks Dame Nature fhews,
And Maidens their Green Sicknefs lofe)
Roger to fhew his Tafte polite,
Mun vifit *Punch* forfooth one Night:
Here, undifturbed by Critic Rules,
And hemm'd by Droves of neighbour Fools,
The Mufic, coarfe-daub'd Scenes and Light,
Cheaply afford our *Hodge* Delight:
At *Punch*'s Smut, which he thought Wit,
His cudden Sides were like to fplit;
And at each Joke, his Lanthorn Jaws
Extended wide, roar loud Applaufe;
Or when Diftrefs aukward appears,
Roger cou'd fcarce refrain from Tears;
The Gothic Story with our Clown,
As Gofpel Truth goes glibly down:—

Not

* This made its Appearance fome Years ago in the *London Magazine.*

Not *Quixotte*'s felf was more deceiv'd,
When *Melifandra*'s Fate he griev'd;
And of the fqueeking pigmy Crew,
His vengeful Sword whole Squadrons flew:----
The Curtain dropt, the Drama ended,
The motley Audience homeward tended,
Clowns, Nurfes, Children, all well pleas'd,
And of their long-ftor'd Farthings eas'd;
While fome more curious than the reft,
Behind the Curtain rudely preft.——
On feeing this, our *Roger* too,
To eafe his Longings needs muft go:
With Fear and Diffidence he enters,
And fcarce to look about him ventures:
Here dangling on a Pin were feen,
A purpled King, or tinfel'd Queen;
Here *Punch* with fceptred Princes tumbled,
Here Priefts with *Beelzebub* lay jumbled;
Here fidelong hanging by a Wire,
A chop-fallen Heroe, Prince, or 'Squire.
With fuch mock Grandeur thus furrounded,
Poor *Hodge*, alas! was quite confounded:——
Twirling his Hat, he fcrapes and bows,
And his Extent of Breeding fhews;——
The reft, at *Hodge*'s droll Miftake,
Laugh 'till their Sides and Midriffs ake:
" Sure, never yet was feen," cries one,
" Such a befotted Simpleton;

" Were

" Were you not blind, you might behold
" 'Tis Tinſel this you take for Gold;
" And what you fancy Fleſh and Blood,
" Is nought, d'ye ſee, but Rags and Wood,
" That cannot ſpeak, look, move, or ſtand,.
" But owes all to the Artiſt's Hand,
" Who fix'd on high, lordly preſides,
" And with a Wire each Action guides."
Roger on this ſeem'd quite amaz'd,
He gap'd, he ſcratch'd his Head, he gaz'd,
While Gybes from every Side accoſt him,
And laughing Boobies coarſely roaſt him;
Each judging of his own great Wit,
By Neighbour *Hodge*'s Want of it.
" Nay, haw'd ye, haw'd ye, where's the Wonder
" That I," quo' *Hodge*, " ſhould make this
                    Blunder ?
" Since, as a Many do report,
" In *London*—nay ſome ſay, at Court,—
" There's nought more common than to ſee
" The Beaver doff'd, and bended Knee,
" To ſtrutting, wooden-headed Beaus,
" With empty Fobbs, and tinſel'd Cloaths;
" Who, Puppet-like, ne'er ſpeak or move,
" But as they're wire-led from above;
" And like theſe Folk aſide are thrown,
" As uſeleſs Logs—*the Work once done*."

                              A RE-

A REFLECTION.

THOU Cherub with a fmiling Face,
Religion! Child of heav'nly Grace,
What Demons, wrapt in horrid Gloom,
Thy Name blafphemoufly affume!

Thro' jaundic'd Eyes Enthufiafts fee
The Image of the Deity;
A Portrait falfe, held up to View
By a defigning impious Crew:
But no *Tartuffe* or ftrolling Widgeon
Shall be my Cat'rer in Religion;
What Reafon dictates, that I'll chufe,
What fhe forbids, I'll ftill refufe;
Shake off the Prejudice of Youth,
And fteer by Reafon's Chart for Truth.

In fpite of *Whitefield* and of *Rome*,
I'll laugh at Superftition's Gloom;
For Modes of Faith will ne'er difpute,
Nor damn a Man for his Surtout;
Deift or Atheift let 'em call me,
And with Cathedral Pellets mawl me,
Threaten with Brimftone, Fire and Hell,
My Cry is—*Vive la Bagatelle.*

Our heav'nly Father never fram'd
Children elected to be damn'd;

Wou'd

Wou'd *Earthly* Parent thus decree?
Can God?---the Thought were Blafphemy;
But Knaves and Fools paint the Almighty
A *Mumbo Jumbo*, to affright ye.

When Nerves relax'd are weather-fhaken,
Spleen' for Religion's oft miftaken;
And then 'tis heav'nly to be fad,
And look moft melancholy mad;
Then comes *Defpair* with *Stygian* Frown,
Impelling Fools to hang or drown:
But *true* Religion foothes the Breaft,
And makes her willing Vot'ries bleft;
Conducts 'em with a fmiling Air,
And banifhes the Fiend *Defpair*.

Our Duty to our God we pay,
In being innocently gay;
That Kindnefs fhewing ftill to others,
From Brother ever due to Brothers;—
(Grant Heaven I never may forget
From Man to Man that focial Debt)
And not to one poor Spot confine
Good-will, which like the Sun fhould fhine
On all alike;—nor Diff'rence fhew
'Twixt Chriftian, Pagan, Turk, or Jew;
For this I hold Religion's Teft,
" Who moft refembles God, worfhips God beft."

H   To

To *Sublunary* Kings Abodes,
How many hundred diff'rent Roads!
And shall we (partial) judge, but one
Muft *Worlds* conduct to *Heav'n's* high Throne?

With sweet Benevolence our Guide,
On future Blifs we may confide;
May, unabfolv'd, attend our Fate,
And Death's grand Summons smiling wait;
On Heav'n's juft Mercy fix Reliance,
And fet Old *Nick* at bold Defiance.

The

The MONK *and* JEW.

A TALE.

TO make new Converts truly bleſt,
A Recipe———*Probatum eſt.*———

Stern *Winter*, clad in Froſt and Snow,
Had now forbad the Streams to flow,
And ſkaited Peaſants ſwiftly glide,
Like Swallows, o'er the ſlippery Tide;
When *Mordecai* (upon whoſe Face
The Synagogue you plain might trace)
Fortune with Smiles deceitful bore,
To a curſt Hole, but late ſkinn'd o'er,
Down plumps the *Jew*, and ſinking found,
Tho' deep the Hole, the diſtant Ground;
Riſing, the friendly Ice he caught,
Which kept him from the chilling Draught;
He gaſp'd——he yell'd a hideous Cry,
No friendly Hand, alas, was nigh,
Save a poor Monk, who quickly ran
To ſnatch from Death the drowning Man.
But when the holy Father ſaw,
A Limb of the *Moſaic* Law,
His Hand outſtretch'd he quick withdrew,
" *For Heav'n's Sake help*"——exclaims the *Jew*;
" Turn Chriſtian firſt," the Father cries,
" *I'm froze to Death*"——the *Jew* replies;

H 2.　　　　　" Froze !

" Froze ! quo' the Monk—too foon you'll know,
" There's Fire enough for *Jews* below:
" Renounce your unbelieving Crew,
" And Help is near"———" *I do—I do :*"
" Damn all your Brethren Great and Small"
" *With all my Heart,—Oh, damn 'em all :*
" *Now help me out*"——" There's fomething more,
" Kifs this bleft Crofs, and Chrift adore ;"
" *There, there—I Chrift adore.*"———" 'Tis well,
" Thus arm'd, Defiance bid to Hell ;
" And yet——another Thing remains
" To guard againft eternal Pains ;
" Do you our Papal Father hold
" Heav'n's Vicar ?——And believe all told
" By holy Church ?"——" *I do, by G—d,*
" *One Moment more I'm Food for Cod ;*——
" *Drag, drag me out,——I freeze,—I die,*"
" Your Peace, my Friend is made on High ;
" Full Abfolution here I give ;
" Saint *Peter* will your Soul receive :——
" Wafh'd clean from Sin, and duly fhriven,
" New Converts always go to Heaven ;
" No Hour for Death fo fit as this ;
" Thus—thus—I launch you into Blifs :"

So faid——The Father in a Trice
His Convert launch'd beneath the Ice.

A G N E S

AGNES' FAST.

A SONG.

I.

'TIS *Agnes'* Fast: The Village Swains
   And *wishing* Nymphs with Care
To see the Semblance of their Mates,
   To drear Church-yards repair.

II.

The whistling Wind and sleety Rain
   Make terrible the Night;
And Darkness with her Negroe Face,
   Ev'n *Parsons* might affright.

III.

Spectres and *Cacodemons* now
   Rove at full Liberty;
For holy *Agnes'* Eve and Fast,
   Is Spectres' Jubilee.

IV.

The Bell strikes Twelve, the Night Owl screams,
   The sheeted Ghosts arise,
While *Susan*——(Wond'rous Force of Love!)
   Straight to the Church-yard hies.

Her

V.

Her Heart young *Roger* long poffeft;
   She fear'd her Mind to break:
For *Sue* young *Roger* long had figh'd,
   Yet fear'd his Love to fpeak.

VI.

" *Hemp-feed I fow, Hemp-feed I reap ;*————
" 'Tis *Agnes*' juft Decree,
" That when in Church-yard thus I fpeak,
" My own True Love I fee."

VII.

Her Incantation fcarcely done,
   Roger appears in View;
The felf-fame Errand *Roger* brought,
   That brought his love-lorn *Sue.*

VIII.

She fcreams, he ftarts, but flies with Speed,
   To clafp her to his Breaft;
And nine Months hence, a little *Hodge,*
   Poor *Sue !*————betrays the reft.

The BEAR *and* GARDINER.

A FABLE.

IN the Days of Old *Pilpay*, there flourish'd a
      Bear,
Good-natur'd and gentle, and quite debonnair;
'Tho' shaggy his Form, yet his Soul was polite,
And to live among Men was Sir *Bruin*'s Delight.
(In those Days, like Men, Bears cou'd reason and
      talk;
At present, like Bears, Men can growl, dance
      or walk :)
This Bear had a Heart which to Friendship
      inclin'd,
And in *Adam* he found a warm Friend to his Mind,
Orestes and *Pylades* were not more kind :——
A Gard'ner was *Adam*, extremely well known,
For his Friendship with *Bruin* in Country and
      Town;
Whenever Friend *Adam* you saw, you might swear
His four-legged Brother wou'd shortly appear;
Or if good Sir *Bruin* you any Time spy'd,
The Gardiner was always observ'd by his Side;
They fed at one Table,—nay further, 'tis said,
(Tho' I can't think that true) they both lay in
      one Bed :

                    With

With Labour o'ercome——In the Shade as one
 Day
Poor *Adam* a fnoring moft happily lay,
Friend *Bruin* fat fquat on his Bum to attend him,
Left during his Sleep Man or Beaft fhou'd offend
 him :
Our Centinel, had not long watch'd, when in
 Scorn,
A monft'rous huge Flefh-Fly came founding his
 Horn ;
In Circles he wing'd round poor *Adam* his Flight,
And lur'd by fweet Vapours, he fain wou'd
 alight ;
On *Adam*'s moift Forehead he fettled,——and
 then——
When beat off——he flew——to his Forehead
 again ;
He buzz'd fo, and teaz'd fo, and ftill was fo
 loud,.
That *Bruin* in Vengeance Deftruction avow'd ;
And cunningly watching, he faw him alight,.
To feaft on the Lips of his Friend as in Spite :
" Oh, ho, quo' Friend *Bruin*, I have you, my
 Dear,
" You foundly fhall pay, by the Lord, for
 your Cheer ;"
And fending, full Drive, a large Stone at the Foe,
He crufh'd him at once with a Death-dealing
 Blow ;

And

And the very next Minute he saw the Fly dead,
He saw all poor *Adam's* Teeth drop from his Head.

    Admit it as a certain Rule;
    Friendship is dang'rous from a Fool.

LIBERTY's ADDRESS *to her* BRITONS, *in*

Behalf of the CORSICANS, 1768.

WITH throbbing Bofom and Woe-fpeaking
     Eye,
On *Albion*'s Sea-beat Shore, poor *Liberty*,
Her Spear thrown, carelefs by her, lay reclin'd,
And gave her Sorrows to the paffing Wind.——

 " Can *Britain*'s Sons with lukewarm Souls
     furvey,
" Th' infiduous *Gaul* thus fpread his Tyrant
     Sway ?——
" Can they, unmov'd, the *Corficans* behold
" To Tyrant *Gaul* like Beafts for Burden fold;
" Thofe Heroes who fo glorioufly have ftood,
" And in *my* Caufe long fhed their richeft Blood?
" Shall *Bourbon*'s haughty Race attempt to bind
" In Slav'ry's galling Fetters, all Mankind?——
" And fhall not my brave Sons like Brethren join
" To fave a World, and blaft the fell Defign?
" Roufe, roufe, ye *Britons*, fee your Crofs difplay'd,
" And to my Favourites wing fraternal Aid;
" Already have they long fuftain'd the Fight,
" And Myriad Foes repeated put to Flight,
" But, ah! in vain—Frefh Myriads onward pour;
" If unfupported, Freedom is no more.
        Butcher'd

" Butcher'd by thefe bafe Sons of Tyranny,
" Who, Slaves themfelves, deteft whoe'er are
    free :———
" In vain the Lion dares the Fight maintain,
" While Myriad Foes befet the hoftile Plain.

  " Wou'd *Britons* but unfheath their conqu'ring
    Sword,
" And friendly Aid in Freedom's Caufe afford,
" The *Gallic* Legions foon wou'd fly the Field,
" And to your dreaded well known Valour yield :
" Roufe, roufe, my Sons :———But ah, I fear,
    (fhe faid)
" The Love of Freedom from your Souls is fled :
" The Fiend, bewitching Luxury———The Son
" Of Slavery, whofe Magic Spells forerun
" His Parent's Steps, his Opiate Influence fheds,
" Unnerves your Hearts, and your weak Coun-
    fels leads ;
" His foft'ning Poifon but prepares the Doom,
" That bury'd in the Duft my darling *Rome.*

  " Oh, fhou'd that fatal Hour, which now I fear,
" (Avert it *Jove* Omnipotent) appear ;
" When Tyranny fhall range with Giant Stride,
" And Barefoot Superftition by her Side ;
" When *Smithfield* Fires again fhall horrid blaze,
" Thofe dire Remembrancers of *Mary*'s Days ;
" When my Fair Offspring *Commerce* fhall depart,
" From her lov'd *Britain* with a heavy Heart ;
      " Shou'd

" Shou'd I again that fatal Moment view,
" To this unhappy Globe I'll bid *adieu.*

   " Like that brave *Greek*,* whofe ever envied
         Name,
" Richly adorns the brighteft Page of Fame;
" Who at *Thermopylæ* refign'd his Breath,
" With Hecatombs of Slaves to grace his Death
" Like him *my* brave *Paoli* dare arife,
" And offer up himfelf a Sacrifice;
" Like him, and the few chofen *Greeks* who fell,
" My felf-devoted Sons their Blood fhall fell,
" And fhew the World that Freedom they *will*
         have,
" Ev'n tho' the Road lies thro' the dreary
         Grave."——

So faid, fhe wing'd her Flight, and difappear'd,
And as fhe flew, thefe Words diftinct were heard
" Confider, partial and miftaken Men;
" Confider——In the *Cyclops* horrid Den,
" The chofen Few (a favourite Repaft)·
" Were but preferv'd, to be devour'd the laft."

      * *Leonidas,* King of *Sparta.*

The

The TRANSFORMATION,

A NORTHERN TALE.*

NEAR to where *Tyne* his Bleſſings ſheds,
    Enriching, as he flows, the Meads,
There liv'd a Monk in Days of Yore,
(*Northumbria*'s Crown when *Cenulph* wore)
Of Life ſevere, and ſpotleſs Fame,
Good Father *Roger* was his Name;
This holy Monk, much giv'n to Pray'r,
Was greatly follow'd by the Fair,
Who ſtill on every ſlight Tranſgreſſion,
To *Roger* flew to make Confeſſion;
Ladies in ev'ry Age we find,
To holy Men are much inclin'd:——

I

A

* An abuſive Poem, called the *Origin of the Newcaſtle Burr*,
publiſh'd a few Years ſince, induced the Author to give the
following to the World: The Story is taken from an old
Record found in a Religious Houſe, on its Diſſolution in the
Reign of *Henry* VIII. and is now in the Poſſeſſion of an eminent Antiquarian not far from *Newcaſtle*.

A truer Saint *Hibernia*'s Shore,
To grace her Annals, never bore;
(*Hibernia!* fam'd beyond the *Nile*,
Of *Holy* Saints the holy Ifle,
Nor does her prefent pious Race
Its *Holy* Anceftry difgrace)
Of Form athletic, yet as mild,
And harmlefs as a new-born Child:
The good Man, *fomehow*, had the Art,
To eafe each female tender Heart;
Whate'er his Penance, ftill content,
They, all Submiffion, underwent.

The lovely *Emma*, faireft feen,
'Mong Maids of Honor to the Queen,
Seem'd chief in his good Graces bleft,
Emma each Day her Sins confeft;
" *Each Day?*" Yes, Sir, each Day;---the Fair
For a long Reck'ning did not care;
She thought it ftill the fafeft Way,
As fhe went on, her Debts to pay;
She chofe not, like your heedlefs Folk,
To get o'er deep in *Satan*'s Book,
Left the black Bill fhould grow too large,
For a poor Maiden to difcharge,
And bring *Old Nick*, fpite of her Honor,
To lay arrefting Hands upon her:——
Your *Maids of Honor* in thofe Days
(So Legends tell us) had ftrange Ways;

They

They put on queer religious Airs,
Frequented Church, and said their Pray'rs;
At least old Writers thus record,
I own I scarce can take their Word,
Considering how politer far,
Our modern *Maids of Honor* are:
But *Satan*, that ill-natur'd Sprite,
Who owes your godly Folks a Spite,
Had manag'd Matters so, that *Emma*
Was brought into a strange Dilemma;
The Monk's Instructions, (strange to tell)
Began to make the *Maiden* swell;
Her Health was turn'd quite turvey-topsey,
She seem'd far gone in Nature's Dropsy.

'Tis a known Axiom in the Schools,
That Love's the Paradice of Fools;
A Paradice, in which is plac'd
A Tree, bewitching to the Taste,
(The *Tree of Knowledge*) which produces
A Fruit replete with poisonous Juices;
This tempts poor Maidens to their cost;
They pluck---and---*Paradice is Lost*;
No longer Happiness dwells there,
'Tis all Repentance---all Despair.

Your sage *Platonists* are inclin'd
To think Love centers in the Mind;

But

But Love a different Story tells,
To Saints, to Sinners, Beaus and Belles.

Poor *Emma*'s tell-tale Looks betray,
That *Emma*'s form'd of yielding Clay;
The Queen enrag'd, infifts on knowing
To what this ftrange Misfortune's owing;
Whilft *Emma*, almoft drown'd in Tears,
With penitential Looks declares,
(The more to fix her Refolution,
Roger had promis'd Abfolution,
Which made her gulph the Lie as free
As tho' it were a Difh of Tea)
" That Father *Bede*, who long had ftrove
" By thoufand Arts to win her Love,
" As on her Couch one Day fhe flept,
" Stole in, and"---here, poor Soul! fhe wept,
Nor more could fpeak!----Each *Maid of Honor*
Difdainfully look'd down upon her;
For virtuous Dames in this agree,
No Crime's like Lofs of Chaftity;
That gone, like a ftruck Deer they fly her,
And think it dang'rous to come nigh her;
One would imagine they were taught,
That Whoring, like the Itch, was caught.

" But who's this *Bede*," the Reader cries,
" The Butt of thefe fame horrid Lies?"
A *Secular*, and one of thofe
Whom Monks avow'd Religion's Foes;

And

And who, tho' hitherto unwed,
Stranger to Joys of Marriage Bed,
Yet held it neither Sin nor Shame
For Prieſts to take a wedded Dame;
While Monks, for Self-Denial fam'd,
Againſt ſuch ſenſual Crimes exclaim'd;
With holy Candle, Book, and Bell,
Damning all married Prieſts to Hell;
Prieſts, who the Papal Power deny'd too,
For which *Old Nick* wou'd thraſh their Hide too.*

No Wonder Monks ſhou'd think it good
To ſhed ſo vile a Sinner's Blood;
If juſt the End which is deſir'd,
No Matter by what Means acquir'd.

Altho' the Monks to *Satan* gave him,
And ſwore not all the Saints cou'd ſave him,
Yet with the Body of the Nation,
Bede ſtood aloft in Reputation;
He taught the Natives to explore
The Sea for Fiſh, the Land for Ore;
'Twas he who firſt the Secret found
Of digging Fewel from the Ground.
Hence Riches, Trade, and many a Bleſſing
Their Children's Children now poſſeſſing;

I 3.   He

---

* It was not 'till ſome Centuries after, that the Pope's
Authority was eſtabliſhed in *England*, and Celibacy in general
enjoin'd the Clergy.

He taught them with a magic Net
The luscious Salmon to beset,
With many other useful Arts,
Which justly won the People's Hearts.

But all his Merit was forgot,
And hid by this unlucky Blot;
A *Maid of Honor* to deflower!
'Twas an Affront to Sov'reign Power;
And *Maids of Honor* ne'er cou'd be
Secure, if *Bede* shou'd go Scot-free:
The Queen declar'd, " She did not know
" How far his Impudence might go;
" And that she thought 'twas monstrous hard
" To take a Lady off her Guard:
" Had she herself been sleeping caught,
" (She trembles at the very Thought)
" Ev'n Majesty she was not sure
" In such a Case wou'd be secure."
'Thus prejudic'd, to the good King
She so describ'd this *Nasty* Thing,
That in his Justice he decreed,
The Culprit for his Crimes shou'd bleed:
" What, die?"---as bad---may Heav'n forefend,
And guard us all from the like *End*;
The blushing Muse cannot for Shame,
In Words *direct* the Thing proclaim;
It was, in fine, the Punishment
Heloise's Lover underwent.

Such

Such was the Monarch's Resolution,
The Time too fix'd for Execution,
The Storm was loud, the Waves ran high,
The Charge direct——vain all Reply.

Of Honor's Gem altho' bereft,
Emma had still some Goodness left;
'Tis true Logicians often paint
Each Woman as a Fiend or Saint;
Whereas a Man is a mix'd Creature,
They say,---of het'rogeneous Nature:
But all these Cobweb airy Fancies
Are little better than Romances;
For Woman, like meer Man, is still
Neither completely good or ill;
A Hodge-podge, Olio, a Podrade,
Of many various Compounds made;
A Mixture form'd of cold and hot,
Of sweet and sour---in short---what not;——
Some strong Ingredient, 'tis confest,
Still to the Palate gives the Zest;
Yet not so pow'rful, but we find
Other Ingredients are combin'd.

There is not in all Nature's Plan
So strange a Paradox as Man;
Man with himself eternal jars,
And wages barb'rous civil Wars :---

Now

Now Reafon---Paffion now prefides,
Whilft diff'rent Limbs take diff'rent Sides;
Againft the Monarch Head, we find
Beneath the Girdle what's confin'd,
In bold Rebellion often rifes,
And the wife Sov'reign's Pow'r defpifes;
And *Amphifbœna*-like, 'tis faid,
We've then at either End an Head:*
When that's the Cafe, we feldom know
To which Head we fhould Homage fhow;
And therefore follow that of Courfe,
Which pulls us with the greater Force.
Poor *Emma*, when fhe firft was Sinner,
Had *Amphifbœna* ftruggling in her.

" What's all this Preachment for?---Go on
" And tell your Tale;"---Good Sir, I've done.

Nor Vice nor Virtue, 'tis moft plain.
In *Emma* bore defpotic Reign;
At firft fhe put on a good Face,
And told her Tale with artful Grace;
But Confcience foon---unmanner'd Gueft!!
Kick'd up a Duft within her Breaft,
And fill'd both waking Thoughts and Dreams
With Brimftone, Hell, and burning Flames;
With.

---

* *Amphifbœna* is a Serpent, faid to have a Head at each End.

With forked Prongs, by horned Fiends
Apply'd to Sinner's hinder Ends;
(A frightful Cafe!---No Lady fure
Such Application cou'd endure)
And all that horrid Apparatus
With which fome fay, the Devil treats us,
When we to vifit him think fit,
And take up Lodgings in his Pit.

No Wonder then that Dreams like thefe
Shou'd pull down Madam on her Knees,
To count her Beads in woeful Plight,
And crofs herfelf from Morn to Night:---
In one of thefe defpairing Strains,
When Fear quite overfets the Brains;
At Midnight Hour, when Fiends prepare
To take a *Frefco* in our Air,
As on her Marrow-bones fhe preft,
Weeping and beating her white Breaft,
A Crow long tam'd, whofe gutt'ral Tone
Had oft diverted *Will* and *John*,
By Chance or Providence convey'd,
Had to our Madam's Chamber ftray'd,
Where fnug as Thief under the Bed,
The Bird conceal'd its Negro Head;
And at the Juncture when the Dame
(Her Thoughts brimful of Fire and Flame)
Addrefs'd her Patron Saint of Wood,
Out pops the Crow, and croaking ftood;

" Have

" Have Mercy, Heav'n---What's this I view,
" 'Tis *Satan's* felf---'tis *Satan's* Hue!---.
" Guard me from Pitchforks and from Hell:"
Croak, quo' the Crow---fhe fcream'd---fhe fell:
The Servants fly, and on the Ground,
Speechlefs the frighted Fair was found;
Reviv'd, fhe raves---" Protect and fave me,
" Let not yon ugly *Satan* have me;
" His faucer Eyes and frightful Tone"---
Another Croak---and down fhe's gone.
The Servants fee the droll Miftake,
And quick to Life their Lady wake:
She ftraightway calls out for a Prieft,
To whom her Sins are foon confeft:
On *Roger's* Wiles fhe throws the Blame
Of all her Crimes---and all her Shame;
And hopes it is not yet too late
To hinder *Bede's* unhappy Fate.

The Queen of this great Change inform'd,
Againft the Monk now loudly ftorm'd:
The King in Juftice too decreed,
That *Bede* fhou'd inftantly be freed;
And that the Compliment defign'd
For *Him*, to *Roger* be affign'd.---

No fooner order'd than 'twas done,
And—whip—his *Sanctity* is gone;

Fog

For after being *Abelarded*,
And from the Court with Shame difcarded,
His Crime appear'd fo very black,
Each Female Friend now turn'd her Back;
For from a Confeffor diffected,
No Comfort fure can be expected.

When Birds fly, or when Veffels fail,
They're always guided from the Tail,
And Cafuifts fay, this is the Cafe
In gen'ral, with the human Race:
The Rudder loft, what follows then?—
Ruin to Ships, to Birds, and Men.

And now, no longer Fortune's Sport,
In Triumph *Bede* was brought to Court,
Where 'having humbly on his Knee
Due Homage paid to Majefty,
He then, in Gratitude as bound,
To Heav'n fell proftrate on the Ground,
That gracioufly had heard his Pray'rs,
And refcu'd him from monkifh Snares;
Nor was his croaking Friend forgot,
A leading Actor in the Plot,
Who, at her Majefty's Requeft,
Shew'd its fine Shapes among the reft:
" May Heav'n's beft Benifon," he cries,
(With Tears of Raptures in his Eyes)
" For

" For ever and for ever fall
"'On King, Queen, *Emma*,—Crow—and all."

 So faid; when Wonderful————but hold,
'Twere neceffary you were told,
That in the Records of that Age,
Miracles crowd in ev'ry Page;
Tho' now-a-days, I know not why,
Nor Miracles or Saints we fpy;——
In fhort—a Miracle uncommon—
Up ftarts the Crow—a lovely Woman;
Young, blooming, handfome, debonnair,
And what's ftill ftranger, wond'rous *Fair*.
To pleafe *Pygmalion*, as 'tis faid,
A Marble melted to a Maid;
And furely, if a Heathen cou'd
Infpire a Stone with Flefh and Blood,
We need fhew little Admiration,
At Madam *Croaker*'s Transformation.

 With Wonder ftruck, while all around
In Silence gaz'd, a Voice profound,
Melodious as a Seraph Sound,
Was heard:——
" Accept, O *Bede*, the Gift Heav'n fends,
" The beft of Wives, and beft of Friends;
" Of ev'ry female Charm poffeft,
" With ev'ry focial Virtue bleft:
" Nor yet defpife her for her Birth,
" What are ye all but Sons of Earth?
       " That

" That Origin cannot be mean,
" Where Heav'n's *immediate* Hand is feen;
" And that the Miracle here fhown,
" To future Times be handed down,
" A lafting Monument of Favor,
" Your Offspring to diftinguifh ever,
" A *Spice* of Mother's *gutt'ral* Tone,
" To Time's remoteft Ages known
" By Name of BURR---fhall mark their Tongue,
" And proudly trumpet whence they fprung;
" A rough, bold Accent, free from Art,
" True *Emblem* of an *honeft Heart*,
" A Mark by which Mankind fhall trace
" Your num'rous, warlike, envied Race;
" Whofe Deeds, not Words, their Fame fhall
" fpread,
" And *Britain*'s Foes their Valour dread."

The Prieft with Rapture Heav'n obey'd,
And wed the lovely, new-form'd Maid;
The Monarch too, gen'rous and kind,
To *Bede* and to his Heirs confign'd
That fertile Track which *Tyne* furveys,
As his broad Stream he proud difplays;
Where Riches flow with every Tide,
And Trade and Liberty prefide :——
Here firft he plann'd that kind Retreat,
(At prefent Induftry's lov'd Seat)
Yclep'd *Newcaftle*;---where the Prieft
To an old Age liv'd highly bleft

K

With

With his *Fair* Spouse :---And 'tis agreed
She brought the Parson such a Breed
(Parsons, we know, are in their Natures
Beyond most. Men, prolific Creatures)
Of little *Bedes*,——that all around
The Parson's Prowess did resound.

'Tis thought this same prolific Power
Remains among them to this Hour;
A num'rous Race; who still inherit
Their Mother's BURR, and Father's *Merit*;
And which distinguishes the Breed
Of Mother CROW and Father BEDE.*

* The *Bede* mentioned in the above is not the same
with the Venerable *Bede*, who liv'd rather earlier than the
Hero of our Tale.

On hearing that Mrs M———, of the Y——
Theatre, was dead.

TO ſhew th' admiring World what Pow'r
    divine,
When Muſic, Beauty, Feeling, all combine,
Cecilia from the Star-pav'd Realms above,
In *M----*'s Form inſpir'd Mankind with Love;—
Alas! her Stay how ſhort! Th' angelic Choir,
Ardent, *Cecilia*'s wiſh'd Return deſire :
The Saint the heav'nly Mandate ſtraight obeys,
And, ſmiling, Heav'n regain'd, to ſing *Jehovah*'s
    Praiſe.

✿✿✿✿✿✿✿✿✿✿✿✿✿✿✿✿✿✿✿✿✿✿✿✿✿✿

On hearing the above contradicted.

IN Mercy to Mankind, relenting Heav'n
  Cecilia to our Pray'rs has longer giv'n;
Death aim'd the Stroke, but quickly dropt the
    Dart,
And Pity, for the firſt Time, touch'd his Heart.

K 3   *From*

From a young SAILOR *to the fame* LADY.

WOU'D fmiling Love propitious trim
my Sails,
And Fortune blefs me with her favourite Gales,
No greater Blifs cou'd my fmall Bark betide,
Than fafe from Storms in *P—t-M——* to ride.

WIT *and* RICHES.

THE Man who Store of *Wealth* can boaft,
In *Wit* will ever rule the Roaft;
His Claim who dares difpute?

Plutus can purchafe *Wit*, 'tis true;
Can *Phœbus* purchafe *Riches* too?
Truth blufhes,---and is *mute.*

The TWO PAPER KITES.

A FABLE.

(Addreſſed to a young Gentleman at School.)

TWO Paper Kites, ballanc'd on high,
    With flaming Lanthorns grac'd the Sky,
While Crowds below admire the Glare,
And think each Light a blazing Star:
Cries one of theſe Night Birds, with Pride,
(The other flutt'ring by his Side)
" Left to ourſelves, Brother, we might
" Above theſe Regions wing our Flight,
" Spurn theſe poor Earth-encircling Skies,
" And to the Lunar World upriſe;
" Like Comets ſhine in yonder Sphere,
" And ſee—what Folks were doing there;
" But theſe curſt Cords, by which we're
        " bound,
" Genius and Worth like ours confound:
" One Struggle, ſpirited, might free,
" And give us both our Liberty;
" Uncurb'd we ſafely then might rove,
" And laugh at Earth-Worms from above."

" Hold, not ſo faſt," replies the other,
" Think, think a little, my good Brother;
" To theſe Reſtraints you ſo deſpiſe,
" We owe the very Power to riſe:
" Without

" Without their Help we might remain
" Unnotic'd Nothings on the Plain;
" Or worfe—on furious Tempefts born,
" We fhould be hurried, dafh'd, and torn:
" Tho' Paper Kites were made to fly,
" Cords were defign'd to hold them by,
" And thofe by whom we're guided know
" How far with Safety we may go:
" Ballanc'd by them we thus afpire,
" While wond'ring Crowds our Blaze admire."

The felf-fufficient Kite with Sneer,
Laugh'd at this over-cautious Fear,
When a brifk Gale that Inftant rifing,
His Friend's Intreaties too defpifing,
With one fmart Jerk his Hold he broke,
And flew before the Wind like Smoak;
Now here—now there—hurried and toft,
He falls to Earth, torn, dafh'd, and loft;
While his more wife and happy Friend,
A diff'rent Praife and Fate attend;
By Prudence held, fecure he flies,
A Meteor to admiring Eyes.

If, *Marcus*, you confider right,
You're little better than a Kite;
Quite volatile, and by the bye,
A fhandy Tenant of the Sky;
And all the Excellence you fhow,
To *Lucius*' prudent Care you owe.

Shou'd

Shou'd you your Tutor's Guidance fcorn,
By Paffion's furious Tempeft born,
Hurry'd and loft on Folly's Shore,
You'll fall---alas!---to rife no more:
But guided by his fkilful Hand,
You'll foar,---an Honour to the Land;
Beam Bleffings from your high-born Station,
And fhine the Star of an applauding Nation.

Written

Written on the GRAVE *of a very beautiful* LADY, *who died of the* SMALL-POX.*

DEEPLY interr'd beneath this Sod is
A Piece of *Dirt*, once call'd a *Goddess* ;
Cou'd you the *Goddess* now survey,
You'd turn disgustfully away :
Here *Putrefaction*'s Brood appears,
And the proud Maggot domineers ;
Those Eyes, than *Phœbus*' Beams more bright,
Now darker than the darkest Night ;
Her Lips, her Neck, her Breasts——alas!
Her all——one foul and putrid Mass.

How near to Beauty's 'witching Pride
Is foul *Deformity* ally'd !
From *Putrefaction*'s fertile Bed
The Rose uprears his fragrant Head ;
From the same fœtid Dunghill too,
The stinking Henbane starts to view ;
All earthly Things beneath the Skies,
From *Putrefaction*'s Source arise ;
A while they flourish and are vain,
And then to Dirt revert again :

What Changes Nature's Monades wear!
Now Fair is Foul—now Foul is Fair :

The

* See Page 47.

The *Putrefaction* of a Clown
May rife again, and wear a Crown;
And He who Millions now commands,
May——" *Whiftle o'er the furrow'd Lands.*"

Ye *Mortal Goddeffes*, be wife,
Beauty juft fhews itfelf and dies;
Hither, O hither come—and fee
What every *Goddefs* foon muft be.

THOUGHTS

THOUGHTS *on reading two Modern Celebrated*
NOVELS.

COU'D we in fpite of Heav'n and Fate,
Our Paffions quite eradicate;
The Fountain then were ftopp'd, from whence
Virtue and Vice their Streams difpenfe.

Never was Picture yet pourtray'd,
Without a blended Light and Shade;
And where the Outline's but expreft,
'Tis a meer lifelefs Piece at beft.

Body and Soul united ftill
Are neither perfect Good or Ill;
Then let us view with pitying Eyes
Shades which from Imperfection rife;
On our own Paffions keep ftrict Guard,
Nor flack too much, nor pull too hard;
Secure, we thus Life's Courfe may take,
Ev'n tho' a Trip we fometimes make.

From the fame Heav'n-implanted Root,
Both Good and Evil jointly fhoot;
Thus on *Caffiva*'s Tree, we know,
Both Nourifhment and Poifon grow.

Well fare thofe Souls fo wond'rous pure,
That human Frailties can't endure;

Such,

'Such Beings were by Heav'n defign'd
For other Planets more refin'd;
But having mifs'd their deftin'd Road,
Were forc'd on Earth to make abode.

A *Sophy* for this World was made;
A fhadelefs *Harlowe* hither ftray'd.

C L E-

CLEORA.

BID all Mankind bow to One ſovereign Lord,
And never more unſheathe the vengeful
  Sword;
On *Greenland*'s Coaſt bid *Indian* Spices bloom,
The Owl confront the Sun with Eagle Plume;
Bid yonder floating Sea, aloft in Air,
Higher upriſe, and ſkim the Lunar Sphere;
Bid Time, at thy Command, obedient ſtay,
Count all thoſe Motes, that in the Sun-Beams
  play;
With eager Haſte the fading Rainbow ſeize,
Or with your Finger ſtop the Tide-ſwoln Seas:
Wild with Deſire, a motley Cloud embrace,
And ſtamp it with a numerous living Race;*
Bid the launch'd Thunder like an Earth-worm
  creep,
Or drag reflected *Dian* from the Deep:
All this you ſooner may effect, than find
The Meteor Changes of *Cleora*'s Mind:
Tir'd with my Search, the Bubble I give o'er,
Yet wiſh ————
Again to dream on *Hope*'s deluſive Shore.

* An Alluſion to *Ixion*'s Amour with a Cloud.

The MOCK HERO.

WHILE *Senisino* with theatric Gait,
 Assumes great *Cæsar*'s Dignity and
   State;
" *Cæsar* ne'er knows what 'tis to fear," he
   cries :——
No sooner spoke,—than straightway from the
   Flies,
A Clump of dangerous Weight comes thun-
   dering down,
Threat'ning Destruction to the Heroe's Crown;
Th' unnerved *Cæsar* trembling straight appears,
He faulters, stammers, and---dissolves in *Tears:*---
Learn, *Britons*, hence, ne'er to assume a Part,
That Nature cries----*Is foreign to the Heart.*

The

The DEVIL DISAPPOINTED.
1746.

WHEN *Satan* firſt heard of the Popiſh
    Invaſion,
And Prieſtcraft and Slavery threat'ned the Nation,
He order'd *Ignatius* and *Lewis le Grand*,
With *Bonner* and *Peters* to wait his Command:
They, cringing and licking his Hoofs, ſoon appear,
While *Nick* ſmiling ghaſtly, cries out with a
    Sneer,
" Here, Scoundrels, here's News will make you
    " look gay,
" All *Europe* muſt ſhortly acknowledge my Sway;
" Young *Charley* bids fair for the Throne of
    " *Great-Britain*,
" Which if he but once has the Fortune to ſit on,
" From theſe darkſome Regions below I'll remove,
" And jointly with him rule Old *England* above:
" From Whipping and Flogging a while I re-
    " leaſe ye,
" And what, I am certain, ſtill better will pleaſe ye,
" With Heretick Blood you may now ſtuff and
    " gorge,
" Drink Popery's Health, and Confuſion to
    " *George*:
" *Rantum Scantum*, ye Dogs, away and rejoice,
" And make Hell reſound with your Hollowing
    " and Noiſe:"

        Soon

Soon faid and foon done:---Away they are flown,
And the News thro' all Hell in a Moment is
       known;
On which, fuch ftrange Rackets and Shoutings
      did follow,
The Devil himfelf could fcarce hear his own
      Holloo :——
Popes, Pickpockets, Jefuits, bald-pated Friars,
Whores, Cardinals, Highwaymen, Abbots, and
      Liars,
Commix'd *fans* Diftinction, all bellow'd their
      Zeal—
For *George*'s Confufion, and Hell's Common-weal.
Some Weeks thus elaps'd, when a Courier came
      quick,
By the Soul of a Jefuit—(Poft) to Old *Nick*;
To the Prefence when brought, he was order'd
      to tell
All he knew 'till his *happy* Admiffion in Hell:
" What News his good Viceroy, the Pope, had
    " fent greeting,
" With whom in a fhort Time he hop'd for a
    " Meeting :
" Tho' Lying of all Things his Highnefs admir'd,
" The Truth, and Nought elfe, at this Time he
    " requir'd."
The Jefuit on this moft fubmiffively fhew'd,
That fpeaking the Truth was quite out of his Road;

                        But

But to pleafe his black Highnefs for once he
 wou'd try,
To tell what had happen'd without the leaft Lie:
With *Charles*'s Landing at *Skie* he began,
Told *Edin*'s* Surrender, and fam'd *Prefton-Pan:*
On taking *Carlifle* and the *Lancafhire* Rout,
Nick chuckled for Joy, and Hell fet up a Shout:
But foon as Prince *William* was nam'd, our
 young *Mars,*
Their Horns were drawn in, and each Fiend
 hung an A-fe:——
" That ill-boding Name," cries Old *Nick*, in a
 Fright,
" Brings frefh to my Mind that damn'd Year
 " *Eighty-Eight :*"
But, Lord! when he'd heard what ftrange Work
 had been brewing,
How all their wife Schemes had brought on their
 own Ruin;
How *William* had conquer'd, and *Charley* had fled,
Poor Devil! he chang'd to the Colour of *Lead:*
He blafphem'd, and damning the Tongue that
 had told him,
Flew raging about fo, that Hell cou'd fcarce
 hold him;
While all his Toad-eating and Hoof-licking Crew,
Like Sheep-Biters fneaking, to Corners withdrew:
       " Are

---

* *Edina*; *Edinburgh* fo called.

" Are all my great Hopes," roars Old *Belzy,*
  " blown over?

" Deſtroy'd by this Heretic Houſe of *Hanover?*

" Shall Pop'ry and Slav'ry no more rear their
   " Head,

" And over Old *England* my Influence ſpread?—

" No more like myſelf Papal Bulls roar aloud?"

" Nor Jeſuits, like Mountebanks, play on the
   " Crowd?

" Shall *Smithfield* Burnt-Off'rings no more ſhew
   " my Sway,

" Nor *Britons* to Power deſpotic give Way?

" In ſpite of my Arts, and my beſt Ally *France,*

" Shall Freedom and Trade ſtill in *England*
   " advance?"

" Religion ſtill flouriſh, and over the Main,

" With Glory unmatch'd, *Britiſh* Navies ſtill
   reign?"

" Shall *Brunſwick,* whom next to my Maker I
   " hate,

" Still govern Mankind, and my Projects defeat?

" Zoons, Brimſtone and Fury! I vow and de-
   " clare it,

" Fleſh and Blood,—nay the Devil himſelf can-
   " not bear it."

So ſaying, half-ſpent, to his Dungeon he crept,

Got drunk with *French* Brandy;---belch'd, f-rt-d
   and ſlept.

       The

The PATRIOTS.

IN feventeen Hundred Forty-five,
When black Rebellion was alive,
And with a Giant Stride came forth,
From her bleak Den, the ftormy North;
Jack, who by Creditors unkind,
Had long in Prifon been confin'd,
As at the Window Bars he ftood,
To take the Air in thoughtful Mood,
Who fhou'd pafs by in martial Geer,
But fwagg'ring *Tom* the Grenadier:—
"Hollo!—now *Thomas*—What's the Crack?"
Cries *Thomas*—"Bad enough, Friend Jack:
" *They fay—(damn him!)—the Young Pretender,*
" *Bids fair to be our Faith's Defender;*
" *And that the Rebels have great Hope,*
" *To bring in* Charley *and the Pope.*"
Quo' *Jack*, with lengthen'd, rueful Face,
" Good Heav'n forbid:—If that's the Cafe,
" *Our Liberty is gone,*—and we
" Muft, *Frenchmen*-like, bear Slavery."
" *Our Liberty!*" cries *Tom,* "*What's worfe,*
" *A thoufand Times a greater Curfe;*
" *If the Pretender mounts the Throne,*
" *Damme—*Our dear Religion's gone."

Thus

Thus *Jack* in Jail exclaims and fears
Freedom will be abolifh'd;
While fwagg'ring *Tom*, Soldier-like, fwears,
The Church will be demolifh'd.

CHARTRES's APOTHEOSIS.

WHEN *Chartres*, his Corpfe not yet cold,
  was to Hell come,
With a Sneer, cries Old *Nick*, " My dear Bro-
  ther! you're welcome;
" 'Mongft the damn'deft of damnable Fools fee
  " him taken,
" Let his Cell be well heated, and finge his old
  " Bacon :"
" 'Mongft Fools!" quite furpriz'd, cries the
  grim-looking Elf,
" Your Highnefs miftakes; I'm a Rogue like
  " yourfelf."—
" To my Coft I have found," replies *Nick*, " 'tis
  " a Rule,
" Tho' Fools may'nt be Rogues, yet *each Rogue's*
  " *a damn'd Fool.*"

BUT.

B U T.

A FABLE.

*E*NVY, a Spectre, frightful, thin,
  The Darling Progeny of Sin;
(Her Sire, as ancient Poets tell,
The lowest, meanest Fiend of Hell;)
A bleer-ey'd Hagg, whose only Food
Is human Hearts and human Blood;
And in her Mouth, instead of Tongue,
Ten Thousand poison'd Arrows hung:
Long had this pestilential Foe
Peopled King *Satan*'s Realms below,
When his black Highness, as in Duty
Bound to her Goodness and her Beauty,
Pour'd Favours multiplied upon her,
Made her a Maid, or Hagg of Honour;
And order'd *Pride*, his King at Arms,
(No Stranger to Miss *Envy*'s Charms)
To make her out an Ancestry,
Long as a *Welshman*'s Pedigree;
And spite of Truth and Virtue prove,
If possible, she sprung from *Jove.*----
This, Herald-like, *Pride* soon effected,
Nor was her Coat of Arms neglected:
The Shield was sable; the Device,
Three Toads, two Snakes, and twenty Lice;

Three

Three Vipers gnawing at a Breaſt,
Serv'd Madam *Envy* for her Creſt;
In ſhort, the Blaze and the whole Coat,
The Fair One's mighty Worth denote :——
The Fair One!——Let not that perplex,
Females are all of the Fair Sex;
And be they olive, dingy, brown,
They're *Fair Ones* call'd throughout the Town.

The Arms made out, ſome ſmall Diſpute
Aroſe, What Motto beſt wou'd ſuit;
Cries *Envy,* grinning out a Smile,
Which ſpoke her Spleen, and eke her Guile,
" My Motto, Good Friend *Pride*, ſhall be
" Three fav'rite Letters, *B, U, T.*----
" By Hell and all the Fiends below,
" To *But*, that Syllable, I owe
" More helliſh Joys---nay ſtare not, *Pride*,
" Than to all other Words beſide;
" Search the whole Dictionary round,
" No Word ſo envious can be found;
" Aided by *But*, I dare commend,
" And ſtab beneath the Vail of Friend :
" With Praiſe, Suſpicion I diſarm,
" And then comes *But* with helliſh Charm,
" And rankles in the inmoſt Core,
" Pois'ning the Praiſe was giv'n before;---
" Thus Poiſon's beſt in Sweets conceal'd,
" Thus Falſhood's hid beneath Truth's Shield.

" No

" No Word like *But* my Spite conveys,
" *But* be my Motto----*But* my Praise."

Dear ———, my best, my worthiest Friend,
  To you I dedicate this Fable;
Goodness like yours it can't offend,
  Your Hearts so very---veritable.

The TWIN-SISTERS.

I.

FAIR *Chaſtity*, of Lilly Hue,
　　And *Modeſty* like bluſhing Roſe,
New-blown and ſteep'd in Morning Dew,
　In *Clara* ·happily repoſe.

II.

All-gràceful, o'er the Fair One's Cheeks,
　The Emblem Lilly ſhines reveal'd,
While Modeſty Retirement ſeeks
　In Beds of Roſes deep conceal'd.

III.

With brazen Front loud *Impudence*,
　(Of empty Noiſe and Folly ſprung)
From his foul Battery of Offence,
　Planted on *Wit-wou'd*'s coward Tongue

IV.

Attacks fair *Chaſtity*,—in Phraſe
　Thro' which the Coxcomb fully glares;
Such Phraſe the Coward Soul betrays,
　When aim'd at helpleſs Maidens' Ears.

Poor

V.

Poor *Chaſtity* alarm'd, for Aid
  Straight calls upon her Twin-born Friend;
With roſy Enſigns quick diſplay'd,
  Her Siſter's bluſhing Powers attend.

VI.

United, they confound the Foe;
  They come, they ſee, they overcome:*
They hurl, like Lightning, overthrow,
  And ſtrike (Amazement!) *Wit wou'd* dumb.

VII.

In Chains their Captive they confine,
  And to th' applauding World proclaim,
The rude Invader they conſign
  To the opprobrious Cave of Shame.

* Alluding to *Cæſar's Veni, Vidi, Vici.*

M   *The*

The MILL.

A TALE.

BENEATH a Court's luxuriant Skies,
Plant *Honesty**, it fades and dies:
Such tender Plants expire of Course,
Oppos'd to *Influenza*'s Force----
That Court Disease, who from her Wings
A thousand magic Poisons flings:—
Nor in the Church's ample Sphere.
Does *Honesty* much better fare;
Nor in the Law's capacious Round
Is the rich Blossom often found;
These Truths from others I relate,
Nor Court, Church, Law—has been my Fate.

The Tenants to Sir *John* complain,
" The Miller purloins half their Grain:"---
What can be done?---On all his Ground,
This Mill, and *only* this, is found;
With Shame the Pilferer's disgrac'd,
And in his Room another plac'd,
Of Fame unstain'd; by all agreed
A Man right worthy to succeed.

Tempta-

---

* A Flower not uncommon in *English* Gardens.

Temptations numberlefs affail;
This Miller, like the laft, proves frail;
Again the Tenants beg Relief,
Sir *John*'s convinc'd that he's a Thief:---
" In Truth, my Friends, I've been deceiv'd,
" No Man more honeft I believ'd;
" A Miller chufe yourfelves," he cry'd,
" On whom we all may fafe confide;
" But firft his Merits clofely fcan,
" To me 'tis equal who's the Man."

After much tedious Altercation,
They come to a Determination;
A Miller's fix'd on; one whofe Name
Challeng'd the loudeft Blaft of Fame;
The Tenants all in this agree,
" If there's an honeft Man---'tis He."

For fome Time no Complaint was heard,
A Month, or longer, 'tis averr'd;
At length---alas---too true, tho' ftrange,
This *Paragon* began to change;
Sufpicion, as if half afraid,
In doubtful Grumblings Hints convey'd;
Thefe Grumblings every Day increaft,
'Till all the Miller glares confeft:
" The Toll too large-----Their Corn when
      " ground,
" Was, on Return, nor fair or found;
" Their

" Their Flour all mix'd,—scarce Half their Due:
" *The greatest Rogue they ever knew.*"

Once more to good Sir *John* they fly:
Sir *John* soon makes 'em this Reply.

" No farther Change I'll now admit,
" To your own Choice you must submit;
" The Miller whom you thus upbraid,
" *Was* honest 'till a Miller made;
" And honest had continued still,
" But for the Air of that damn'd Mill:
" At that alone your Vengeance aim;
" The Mill and not the Man's to blame."

Learn, Reader, from this little Tale,
That ev'n the best of Men are frail;
And where curst Influenza's *found,*
Millers *will evermore abound.*

The CRITIC and BARD.

A FABLE.

A CRITIC with a Phiz fevere,
   The Quinteſſence of Cynic Sneer,
Who ſtill put on the----*Very Wiſe*,
A Cuckow in an Owl's Diſguiſe;
To while away his vacant Time,
Chanc'd to take up a Book of Rhyme;
Whether the Work of *Dryden, Gay*,
Or *Pope*, we can't exactly. ſay:---
He reads, he ſneers, he drops the Book,
And with a ſelf-ſufficient Look
Thus cries----- " Good Heav'ns! what Stuff
      " is here.?

" Such Nonſenſe Fools alone can bear ;
" Your Poets make their Meadows laugh,
" Their Spears and Swords the Life-Blood quaff;
" The liſt'ning Moon ſtoop from her Sphere,
" Some Lover's Madrigals to hear;
" While Sylphs and Fairies---which ſtill worſe is,
" (Fit Entertainment for old Nurſes)
" Fill idle Brains with fooliſh Fancies,
" Ev'n worſe than *N-b--*'s damn'd Romances :
" One common Sentiment in Proſe,
" Is worth a thouſand Books like thoſe."

He ſpoke; and to his great Surprize,
The Poet's Shade confronts his Eyes :

      " Shall'

" Shall grovelling Pedants Rules impofe,
" And judge of Song by Laws of Profe,
" (Exclaims the Bard),?---Shall Clods afpire,
" Eyelefs, to guide bright Sons of Fire?——
" As well might Owls thro' Blaze of Noon,
" Guide *Jove*'s own Bird to hail the Sun:—
" The *Plaftic* Sifters can with Eafe
" Infpire, create, whene'er they pleafe;
" With Life can Fields, Trees, Floods endue,
" Ev'n all Things---fave fuch Clods as you.

" The *Mufes*' Temple, high in Air,
" Was never form'd by Rule or Square;
" Infpired by the Genial Nine,
" Wild *Fancy* drew the Plan Divine;
" And while they fung their heav'nly Strain,
" To Mufic rofe the magic Fane.

" Be humble, Wretch, thy Spleen controul,
" For know---you're but a Critic Mole;
" And Moles, when *Phœbus* fhines moft bright,
" Are bury'd in the darkeft Night."

So faid, the Bard, frowning Difdain,
Re-melted into Air again:
Th' unfeeling Critic, undifmay'd,
Scarce underftood one Word was faid;
But like his Brethren of all Four,
Thought on---as he had thought before.

On

On being asked by Miss ⸻ to write a RIDDLE.

I.

WHAT is that Thing which Man defires,
  Inform me, Ladies, if you can?
That pleafes moft, yet fooneft tires,
  The Comfort and the Plague of Man?"

II.

That Paradox, which Mortals find
  Sometimes a Truth, oftner a Fiction,
By fage Logicians defin'd,
  An Axiom, yet a Contradiction.

III.

To this fame Being—(ftrange! tho' true)
  We owe our very Prefervation;
And in fome Meafure's likewife due,
  Our Health, our Wealth, nay our Creation.

IV.

The Phantom we approach with Fear,
  Yet carelefs when the Prize is got;
Like *Hamlet*'s Ghoft,---'tis here---'tis there---
  We have it, and we have it not.

To

V.

To play on better than Baſſoon,
   Than Hautboy, Harpſichord, or Fiddle;
Yet, often harſh and out of Tune;——
   What's the ſtrange Name of this ſtrange Riddle?

Cloe enquiring what this Riddle was,
I led the ſmiling Fair One to a Glaſs.

The

The SPLEEN.

I.

ASK *Plumbo*, what's the dreadful Cause,
    That he's so gloomy seen,
Plumbo brings out with labour'd Pause,
    He's tortur'd with the Spleen.

II.

But Dulness and the Spleen, my Friend,
    In Nature differ wide;
Dulness and Folly kindred blend,
    While Wit to Spleen's ally'd.

III.

The Man who with the Spleen's possest,
    Is like an *April* Day;
This Hour by mirky Clouds opprest,
    The next serenely gay.

IV.

Not so the Man, within whose Skull,
    Dulness bears soveriegn Rule;
Like a *November* Day he's dull,
    A *semper idem* Fool.

RIGHT.

RIGHT-HAND and LEFT.

A FABLE.

THE Right-Hand,—'twas but t'other Day,
    Thus to the Left was heard to fay:
" If fome Folks knew themfelves, 'twere well,
" Give 'em an Inch, they'll take an Ell;
" 'Twou'd be with Manners more confiftent,
" If, Sir, you kept a little diftant;
" Tho' now and then I condefcend
" To ufe you as a menial Friend,
" Kindly to clafp, embrace, and fhake ye,
" When frofty Seafons chilly make ye;
" Becaufe forfooth I fometimes ftoop,
" You feem to ride quite Cock a hoop;
" And dare, tho' fo much underbred,
" Equal with me to hold your Head:---
" If to your proper Ufe apply'd,
" You're only fit to wipe B-----e,
" Or fome fuch fervile Work, while I
" The nobleft Scenes of Art fupply:
" By me his Skill each Artift fhows,
" By me the mimic Canvafs glows;
" And what the Sifter Nine indite,
" Were loft, if I, Sir, did not write:

                                 " 'Tis

" 'Tis I who Wisdom's Truths explain,
" I'm premier Midwife to the Brain;
" Lovers by me their Pains reveal,
" The Cards I shuffle, cut and deal:
" But what's superior to the rest,
" What makes me most supremely blest,
" The Fair I'm licens'd to approach,
" To touch, to lead 'em to their Coach;
" Thus blest, 'tis I, Sir, can impart
" Raptures most thrilling to the Heart;
" While you, with Aukwardness disguis'd,
" Are to a Proverb ev'n---despis'd:
" So, good *Sinister*, judge the Sequel,
" You're not to think yourself my Equal."

Sinister, cool and free from Passion,
Thus answer'd *Dexter*, his Relation.

" Good Brother---for say what you will,
" You're only my Twin Brother still;---
" What's all this mighty Fuss about?
" You quite forget yourself, I doubt;---
" In every Thing you undertake
" What a fine Figure you must make
" By me unaided, worthy Sir?----
" You'd look as strange as one-ear'd Cur:
" You know in Quibbling I delight,
" You're sometimes *Wrong*, tho' always *Right*:
" In

" In every Monument of Art,
" I never fail to bear a Part;
" The *Muſes'* Bus'neſs I cou'd do
" Upon a Pinch, as well as you;
" And with the Fair, the Hand that gives
" The Heart, and mutually receives,
" Or Right or Left, 'tis all the ſame;
" Such Trifles burning Hearts diſclaim:
" In Dancing too---nay, never ſtare,
" Right-Hand and Left my Worth declare;
" And *Hoyle* himſelf, without my Aid,
" Would find Quadrille an aukward Trade.

" Thoſe great Advantages you boaſt,
" Are accidental at the moſt;
" To Education they are due,
" Not to intrinſic Worth in you:
" With equal Talents born, had I
" Been *taught* my Talents to apply,
" You had not call'd me your Inferior,
" But, envious, found me your Superior;
" For Envy in that Breaſt muſt dwell,
" That with Pride's Meanneſs thus can ſwell.

" What's yours, Chance might have made
    " another's;
" Tho' Right and Left we ſtill are Brothers."

How ſweeter far the Garden Roſe,
To that which in the Hedges grows!

How

How diff'rent *Afric*'s tawny Race,
From thofe who *Europe*'s Climates grace!
Tho' Nature the Foundation lays,
Art muft the Superftructure raife;
And the Criterion of each Station,
Proceeds alone from Education.

A S O N G.

I.

HOW wretched is your Lover's Fate,
I die with Grief if you fhou'd hate;
If to my utmoft Wifhes kind,
Death from Excefs of Joy I find.

II.

Since either Way I Death muft know,
Let it, dear Nymph, from Kindnefs flow;
Such Death more joyous I'd receive,
Than any Life that Heav'n can give.

The TWO CANDLES.

A FABLE.

TWO Candles burning in a Hall,
    The one large-wick'd, the other small;
While Large-Wick chearful blaz'd and bright,
The other scarce gave any Light;
But in a Corner on a Shelf,
Just glimmer'd, as to please himself:—
Cries Small-Wick, sneering, to the other,
" You blaze away, my showy Brother,
" But that superior Light you boast
" Must soon---so quick you burn---be lost;
" While, to Self-preservation true,
" I shall out-live three such as you:
Large-Wick, directed by the Sound,
His dark'd-ey'd Neighbour quickly found,
(Who else must have unnotic'd been,
And, as quite worthless, overseen)
And thus reply'd: " Thou gloomy Aid
" To the dark Us'rer's baneful Trade;
" Thou *Darkness visible*, scarce seen,
" Thou fit Companion for the Spleen;
" From thy poor Gasconade desist,
" Yours is not Life—you but *Exist*;

       " While

" While I, the few ſhort Hours I know,
" In doing Good my Time beſtow;
" Candles are deſtin'd to ſupply
" The Want of Day-light in the Sky;
" Like ſupplimental Suns to light,
" And baniſh Darkneſs, Gloom, and Night;
" To lengthen Life, and kindly' ſhower
" That Bliſs of Bliſſes, Viſual Power:
" This, while I live, I cheerful do,
" While ſuch poor ſelfiſh Things as you,
" Who hugger-mugger ſpend your Rays,
" And have not Soul to give a Blaze,
" Are ſtill unnotic'd by Mankind,
" But when you leave a Stink behind."

' The Conteſt *Suſan* heard, and took
Small-Wick from his ſequeſter'd Nook;
She thruſt him in the Kitchen Fire,
Worthleſs,---unheeded---to expire:
While Large-Wick, in the Parlour grac'd,
And 'mid ſurrounding Beauties plac'd,
A cheerful Luſtre boldly throws,
And to the laſt his Spirit ſhows.

Souls are like Candle-Wicks---when ſmall,
They ſcarce give any Light at all:
When large---they're public Bleſſings found,
And beam their cheerful Blaze around;

And

And if our Lives, as Sages ſhow,
Are meaſur'd by the Good we do,
And not by Days and Months----I fear
Too many Small-Wicks will appear;
And may be ſaid, with Truth's Conſiſtence,
Barely to know the *Twilight of Exiſtence.*

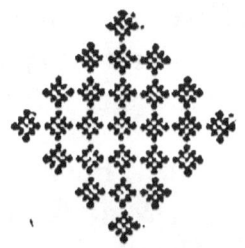

ABUSE and FLATTERY.

LIKE Hail, that ſtrikes with Force, yet
    leaves no Wound,
But harmleſs falls, and waſtes upon the Ground;
Abuſe, when undeſerv'd, we ſafe abide,
Her Arrows conſcious Virtue turns aſide:
But ah!---like Rain that gently falling, cleaves,
While the drench'd Garb the dang'rous Gueſt
    receives;
Flatt'ry, ſoft ſtealing, eaſy Entrance finds,
And proves the Bane of unſuſpecting Minds:
To the Soul's Core the Phantom ſteals unknown,
Health flies, and Fever fills the vacant Throne;
Raving a while we ſkim a Fairy Coaſt,
Nor from th' Illuſion wake, 'till we are loſt.

When Vice the honeſt Boſom wou'd enſnare,
The Flatterer's *Janus* Maſk ſhe's ſure to wear;
And as our Body's Health the Rain annoys,
Flattery's inſiduous Dew our Souls deſtroys.

The O P I F E R.

*P*HOEBUS, as Poets all aver,
   Is Nature's grandeſt *Opifer* :
They ſay, that ev'ry Thing we view
To his inſpiring Pow'r is due;
That he impregnates Mother Earth,
To ev'ry Flow'r and Tree gives Birth;
That he alone can *vivify*,
(A monſt'rous Falſhood by the Bye!)
For marvellous as Poets ſhow him,
Cloe a Bar's Length can out-do him.

   When *Phœbus*, by his *genial* Power,
Wakes into Life each Herb and Flower,
What Days and Weeks and Months are fled,
E'er Vegetation rears its Head!
Slow into Life the Flowers creep,
And grow as they were half aſleep;
But when fair *Cloe* moves along,
Like Lightning ſtarts a new-made Throng;
The Flow'rs beneath her Feet ſhoot high,
As if ſome Wonder to eſpy;
Which, plain as Pike Staff, muſt denote
A Something in her Petticoat,
That makes glad Nature quicker riſe,
Than all th' *Apollos* in the Skies.

                And

And did not *Cloe* nimbly pafs
Over the animated Grafs,
The fportive Flow'rs wou'd joyous fhow,
By grateful Kiffes what they owe,
To that fame *vivifying* Part,
Which fuch ftrange Magic can impart.

Written

t.

Written in a Company where DETRACTION
engroſſed the Converſation.

I.

SWEET to the Scent's the ſmelling Briar;
 Yet touch'd it gives us Pain;.
The Streamlet we ſo much admire,
 Is oft diſtain'd with Rain.

II.

The Painting that delights the Eye,
 To Shades its Beauty owes;
On the ſame Shrub conjoin'd we ſpy
 The Thorn and bluſhing Roſe.

III.

No Mortal ever yet was made
 From Imperfection free;
Angels themſelves have ſome ſmall Shade;----
 Heav'n wills it thus ſhou'd be.

IV.

Mercy to others Failings ſhow,
 As you wou'd be forgiv'n;
The beſt Man's Lot, alas, were Woe,
 Were Mercy not in Heaven.

The

The FLOCK of WILD-GEESE.*

CROSSING the *Humber* in a Wherry,
  The Weather fine, Companions merry;
The Day, if I can right remember,
The twenty-third of laſt *December*,
An honeſt Farmer chanc'd to ſpy
A Flock of Wild-Geeſe in the Sky;
His Head he eager ſcrats, he grins,
" Look there, Friend *Will*," he cries, " odſwinds!
" Thoſe Wild-Geeſe ſcudding o'er yon Spot,
" Would prove a moſt delightful Shot;
" Were I on Shore and had my Gun,
" By'r Lady, I'd have glorious Fun;
" High as they fly, I'll hawd a Crown,
" I'd bring ſome of their Worſhips down."
Will rubs his Eyes—" Why how now, *Ned*,
" For certain ſure you're wrong i'th' Head---
" Wild Geeſe! I've look'd and look'd again——
" Are not theſe Wild-Geeſe in your Brain?
" My Eyes, thank Heav'n are ſtrong and clear,
" And yet no Geeſe to me appear:"
" Quo' *Ned*, " Your Sight is woundy dim,
" See—o'er yon Mill—there—there they ſkim;"
                                 Will

---

* The above was written on being applied to by two Diſ-
putants; one of whom was warm in Praiſe of *Triſtram Shandy*,
and the other abuſing it as a Work of no Merit.

Will fwears " There's nae fike Thing: That he
" As well as any Mon can fee;"
While *Ned*, to Anger half inclin'd,
Re-fwears—" That Farmer *Will* is blind:"
Hot and more hot grows the Difpute;
The other Paffengers are mute:
High Betts are offer'd——fure Decifion,
To prove each right in his Opinion.—
At length, unable to agree,
They make Old *Hobfon* Referee;
Determined by his Voice to reft,
Which of the Two could fee the beft.
Cries *Hobfon* with fagacious Look,
(His Beard down-ftroaking as he fpoke)
" *Ned* fwore he faw—nay fwears it ftill,
" A Flock of Geefe o'er yonder Mill:
" This *Will* with Trooper Oaths denies,
" While *Ned* fwears, *Will* has got no Eyes;
" *Will* might with Modefty have faid,
" He nothing faw;——and Farmer *Ned*
" Inftead of flying thus outright,
" Shou'd have compaffion'd *William*'s Sight.
" That *Will*'s quite honeft I believe,
" But Eyes fhort-fighted will deceive;
" And all *Will*'s Oaths but barely fhow,
" That *Ned* fees farther of the Two.
" Shake Hands---be Friends---let Difcord ceafe,
" And o'er a Tankard fign your Peace.

Thus

Thus *Hobfon*—But fhort-fighted *Will*
Perfifts in his Opinion ftill.

None are more *obftinate* than thofe
Who can't fee farther than their Nofe;
And Moles are of that ftupid Kind,
They don't perceive that they are blind.

The

The WIT's PROGRESS.

YOUR Genealogifts decide,
 That Wit to Folly's near ally'd;
Whence 'tis obferv'd, that Senfe and Wit,
In friendly Union feldom hit.

At *Macro's* Birth each Goffip cries,
"She fees Wit fparkle in his Eyes;"
Ev'n at the Breaft his Wit amazes,
And Nurfe is lavifh of her Praifes;
Whether he laughs, or cries, or crows,
Uncommon Wit her Baby fhows:
But one Thing makes poor Nurfy grieve,
"She fears he'as too much Wit to live."

At School he Learning quickly gains,
Yet feldom what he gets retains:
Mifchief is *Macro's* chief Delight,
Mifchief he ftudies Day and Night;
And he who Mifchief beft can hit,
With School-Boys is the greateft Wit.
But even in thofe boyifh Days,
His Breeches' Tenant often pays,
For Mafter *Macro's* witty Ways;
Sure Prologue to the many Woes
His ripen'd Wit muft yet difclofe.

At

At College each raw Youth is smit
With *Macro's* Humour, Whim, and Wit;
By which his Vanity's encreaft;
He thinks himfelf a *Swift* at 'leaft;
But *Macro's* fo amazing quick,
To One Thing he can never ftick:
Meer Superficials fuffice;
Macro's too witty to be wife:
Of each Preceptor and grave Soph,
His Wit is fure to make a Scoff;
With him each Fellow's an Old Mifs,
Of *Mafculini Generis:*
From *Locke* or *Newton* fee him run,
With Pleafure to enjoy a Pun;
And all the Senfe of *Ariftotle*
Is a meer Trifle to a Bottle:
This foon brings on the Art of Drinking,
To 'which fucceeds the Want of Thinking;
For when Wit owns the Bottle's Sway,
Poor Wit's in a confumptive Way:
He drinks, he games, he wenches, fwears,
And a moft glorious Buck appears.

Expell'd from College, *Macro* foon
Among the *Bedford* Wits is known;
Here Wit is current fure to pafs,
If fix'd with an Alloy of Brafs:
Now like his Brother Wits he dreams
Of Glory and *Pactolean* Streams;

But

But Confequences foon declare
'Tis building Caftles in the Air;
For Wit's an hungry Entertainment,
It feldom brings us Food or Raiment:
He writes and fpins his Cobweb Brains,
Small his Renown, but lefs his Gains:
His flip-fhod *Billingfgate-*fprung Mufe
Is perfect Miftrefs of Abufe:
He libels, and our modeft Bard
Receives a Gudgel for Reward;
His little Patrimony flies,
His Wit brings in but poor Supplies;
At length in Want of Board and Bed,
He Hack'ney Scribbler turns for Bread;
Hunger and ragged Want affail,
And his laft Lodging is a Jail:
Defpis'd by All, and All defpifing,
Not the leaft Spark of Hope arifing;
Like a *True Wit* he ends his Pains,
And *foolifhly* blows out his Brains.

Have you not in a darkfome Night,
A Meteor feen; with rapid Flight
Dart thro' the Sky,—while Blockheads fwear,
The glitt'ring *Nothing* is a Star:
Ended its unfubftantial Fires,
In fome foul Ditch it foon expires.

ONE

O N E.

ONE only Babe that pretty, good and wife
  Now breathes;—and that's *my* Babe each
       Nurfy cries;
One only Faith that points to Heav'n the Way,—
" That Faith *I* preach," you hear each *Fla-*
      nien fay;
" But One True Judgement," cries each *Critic*
    Elf,
And that, he fwears, is center'd in *Himfelf:*
One *Garrick* is the univerfal Cry,
And but One *George* were Treafon to deny;
Miftaken all! Let Emulation warm,
What erft was fingle, into Life will fwarm;
And where prolific Genius ftrikes the Root,
More Flow'rs than One from the ftrong Stem
     will fhoot.
Of all *Created,* there are more than One;
Single there's Nothing, fave—*One God alone.*

The

The WHALE and TUB.
1766.

THE Whale appears, he foams, he rages,
 And Ruin to the Ship prefages;
An empty Tub is quickly thrown,
And lo!—The Monfter's Fury's gone;
And Sir *Leviathan*, with Pleafure,
Plays with his empty wooden Treafure
Like Child with Rattle, and ne'er thinks
Whether the Veffel 'fwims or finks:
Juft fo our Monfter, the huge Rabble,
Who, tublefs, ftill will fight and fquabble,
And of the Nation's Rights talk high,
Of Taxes, Trade, and Liberty;
Muft, to amufe them, have fome Toy,
Their fhallow Noddles to employ;
The Bottle Conjurer, a Ghoft,
Befs Canning, or fome fav'rite Toaft,
Shall, bubble-like, fix their Attention,
And prove a Bone of fierce Contention;
While thofe the Public Helm who fteer,
With Eafe can of the Whale keep clear.

The Public Tub, the reigning Fafhion,
 By which the Whale's Attention's caught,
Is a *huge* Tub to pleafe the Nation,
 From *Patagonian* Highlands brought.

Long may our gracious Monarch live,
And long in Safety may he reign;
And grant that Common Senſe revive,
And *Britons* bear a better Brain.

A NOSTRUM.

TOO fhort *Seven* fleeting Years, to re-fupply
    Thofe *Droves* that by Electioneering die;
But were an Act *Triennial* to take Place,
One fingle Age wou'd murder all our Race:
A *Noftrum* ftill remains,—*Britons,* be wife,
In *Ballotting* this Saving *Noftrum* lies;
The Axe 'tis fixing at Corruption's Root,
Which cut, wou'd venom'd Influence ceafe to
        fhoot;
A Pow'r more ftable Monarchs wou'd attain,
And o'er a free-born, *willing* People reign.*

* Balloting, not only in Elections for Parliament, but
in all National Concerns, from the Chufing a Petty Con-
ftable, to the Decifion of Parliamentary Queftions.

The DIFFERENT MEDIUMS.

*N*ED with his Comrade *Dick* difputes,
   What Simile the apteft fuits,
In ftriking Colours to declare
The various Paffions of the Fair.

  " No Simile fo very pat
" To me appears, as that of—*Cat*,"
Cries *Ned:* " Tho' thoufand Proofs arife,
" A few, I fancy, may fuffice.

  " Women when young, are frifky, gay,
" Quite kittenifh, and full of Play;
" When riper grown in Love or Wit,
" Like Cats they're apt to fcrat and fpit.

  " By ancient Bards it has been faid,
" A Cat was turn'd into a Maid:
" May we not from that Fountain trace
" Our modern fkittifh, cattifh Race?

  " The Fiercenefs of a Cat is feen
" Whene'er you raife a Woman's Spleen;
" This Hour fhe purrs in friendly Note,
" The next fhe faftens on your Throat:
" Still in Extremes, like Cats they fhew,
" Whether they fcrat, or purr, or mew.

'Tis

" 'Tis thought that Cats have got nine Lives:
" Some Husbands think so of their Wives. ,

" In Cats when raging Passions dwell,
" Their Tails like Bottle Brushes swell;
" In Women too, when Rage prevails,
" You're sure to find it"——————

" Blasphemer, hold—(cries *Will*) for Shame!
" Nor thus the Angel-Sex defame:
" If aught beneath high Heav'n can bear
" To stand as Emblem to the Fair,
" The *Dove*—the *Turtle-Dove* alone,
" Must in that favour'd Light be shewn.

" How sweetly Women bill and coo!
" How loving, tender, and how true!
" No Gall finds Room within their Breast,
" *There* Turtle *Love* erects his Nest;
" Ev'n when they most displeas'd appear,
" The Turtle's plaintive Moan we hear.

" When dire Misfortune's baleful Smart,
" Has flutter'd little *Tommy's* Heart,
" In his lov'd Mate he constant finds
" A Sov'reign Balm for wounded Minds;
" She curves, and with encircling Wings
" She looks and acts such tender Things,
" Grief's banish'd,—and the conscious Grove,
" Re-murmurs with their mutual Love:——

" With

" With Dove-like . Sweetnefs thus the Fair
" Guards Man againft the Fiend *Defpair:*
" She fmiles, fhe fpeaks, and each Carefs
" She mixes with fuch Tendernefs,
" Misfortune's Darts no more annoy,
" But all is Love, and rapturous Joy..

 " In Patience Nothing can compare
" With Turtle Doves,—except the Fair..

 " Pray, what are *Venus* and her Doves,
" But Emblems of their Charms and Loves?

 " In fhort, in every Thing they do,
" Whether they murmur, bill or coo,
" Women are Turtles, gallefs, kind and true.

Ned laugh'd aloud; then fighing faid,
" You're fingle, *Dick*——but I am wed."

Thro' different Mediums *to Men's Eyes,*
How widely different Things appear!
 While Juggler Prejudice *fupplies,*
The different Spectacles we wear.

The SWIMMERS.

A Youth of Parts and Genius bright,
   In Swimming took a great Delight;
At fi ft. the Stream he cautious enters,
Nor higher than his Navel ventures;
Short Strokes his Want of Skill denote,
The briny Wave gets down his Throat:——
Determin'd ftill he perfeveres,
Nor Pain or Difficulties fears;
Acquires, each Trial, Something new,
(What will not Perfeverance do?)
'Till by Degrees he boldly braves
With fearlefs Breaft th' oppofing Waves;
Roves at Difcretion, and with Skill,
Or fkims the Stream, or dives at Will;
His School Mates all in this agree,
"No Youth more graceful fwims than he;"
How deep *Hall* cares not Half a F—t,
Quite Mafter of the Swimming Art;
Can found the Depths, and at his Leifure,
Search all the River thro' at Pleafure.

His Comrade *Dick*, the felf-fame Views,
Tho' in a different Road purfues;
Too indolent to perfevere,
Bladders, full blown, his Carcafs bear;
By them up-born, *Dick* long with Pride
Had, Straw-like, floated on the Tide;
With

With Superficials content,
And boaftful wherefoe'er he went;
But *Dick*, alas! cou'd never found
The Depths, nor reach the fathom'd Ground.

One Day as o'er the Stream he hies,
And on his puft-up Friends relies,
Venturing, as Coxcombs often will,
Beyond his Depth—devoid of Skill,——
The Bladders burft,—*Dick* meets his Fate,
And mourns his Want of Skill too late;
With wifhful Eyes he views the Shore,
And finks, alas! to rife no more.

In Learning or in Politics,
How many fuperficial *Dicks!*
While *Halls* to Senfe and Learning true,
Alas!—how very, very few.

None from their Wadings fhould depart,
But Mafters in the Swimming Art.

I N

IN SESE VOLVITUR ANNUS

" WITH fprightly Mein and Vifage bland,
"   In order firft, throughout the Land,
" *Spring* trips it, and where'er fhe treads,
" With Sweets revives the fickly Meads;
" Strews Flowers as fhe fports along,
" And bloffom'd Sprays refound the Song;
" While Man, Beafts, Birds, and Fifh combine,
" In Praife of Genial *Valentine:*
" Playful as Kid, amid her Train,
" Is feen the Village Maid and Swain;
" The *Loves* and *Graces* at her Sight,
" Whom *Winter*'s Chill had put to Flight,
" From Heav'n, accompanied by *Mirth*,
" Again revifit *Spring* and Earth;
" And *Nature*, with a gladfome Eye,
" Beholds her Darling paffing by.

" Next, with that Majefty and Pride
" By which Heav'n's Queen is dignified,
" *Summer* fucceeds—Whofe pow'rful Sway,
" Earth, Seas, and kindling Air obey:
" The Sun from *Cancer* darts his Rays,
" And pours an all-commanding Blaze;
" Impregns with Life the fruitful Earth,
" And all Creation burfts to Birth:——
" On her Left-Hand, with glowing Face,
" *Heat* flowly moves:——With gentle Pace

P   " *Zephir*

" *Zephir* upon her Right is feen,
" Comprefs'd by whom, the melting Queen
" Produc'd fair *Health*, a lovely Boy,
" Whom all admire, yet few enjoy.

" She paffes on—and in her Rear,
" *Autumn*, Shief-crown'd, behold appear;
" And *Plenty* with a buxom Face,
" And *Cheerfulnefs* with fmiling Grace,
" Dance Hand in Hand, and o'er the Plains,
" *Trip to* EUPHROSINE'S *light Strains*;
" While *Ceres*-bleft, the Reaper's Throng
" The Chorus joins of Nature's Song:
" With echoing Horns the Hills refound,
" The Hare flies o'er the fhaven Ground;
" The loaded Waggons ftrip the Fields,
" The founding Flail the Peafant wields,
" Joyous he fills the flowing Bowl,
" And *Pleafantry* infpires each Soul;
" O'er Harveft Suppers gay prefides,
" And, mirthful, fhakes his lufty Sides;
" And *Spleen*, felf-banifh'd, takes her Flight,
" Conceal'd in Darknefs, Gloom, and Night.

" From the bleak North, in Sables dreft,
" Crawls *Winter* laft,—with Age oppreft;
" Blear-ey'd—his Back ybent like Bow,
" His bald Head deeply cap'd in Snow;
" With fhrunk in Cheeks—and frightful Beard
" Of Ificles;—his Voice is heard

" In

" In howling Tempefts—and his 'Train
" Compos'd of Fogs, Winds, Snow, and Rain;
" With fcanty Light, obliquely given
" From the remoteft Part of Heaven :
" His wrinkled Vifage, Looks fevere,
" Strike *Nature* with a chilly Fear;
" Languid her Pulfe and Spirits beat,
" And, frighted, to her Heart retreat :
" Where'er he moves, wild Horror reigns,
" He fpreads Deftruction thro' the Plains,
" 'Till *Hope* once more with Cherub's Wing,
" Points the Return of youthful *Spring*;
" At whofe Approach the Tyrant flies,
" To cheerlefs *Patagonian* Skies ;
" While, as before, in Order due,
" The paffing Seafons we review.

" Thus Nature Annual Life refumes,
" And with frefh Youth and Beauty blooms;
" While all the Changes Mortals know,
" From one poor fingle Round muft flow;
" For wounded once by *Winter*'s Sting,
" Man never hails Return of *Spring*."

Beneath a fpreading Shade reclin'd,
Thus *Lucius* fung with penfive Mind;
When bleft with Mufic's fweeteft Lay,
A heav'nly Voice was heard to fay:
" Can Man, ungrateful, thus defpair?
" Man, who is Heav'n's peculiar Care:

" Reafon

" Reafon and Revelation fhow,
" That Man, Heaven-favour'd Man, fhall know
" Another Spring above the Skies,
" Where like a *Phœnix* he fhall rife,
" Where gloomy *Winter* never comes,
" But *Spring* unfading always blooms;
" And He who *Virtue*'s Mount can climb,
" Defiance bids to murd'ring Time:
" The Seafons which in Orbits run,
" The Earth, and Heav'n's great Eye, the Sun,
" Yon azure Vault, and Starry Hoft,
" Shall fade---again in Chaos loft:
" Ev'n Time itfelf fhall be no more,
" While *Virtue* fhall immortal foar;
" For *Virtue*'s Stream can never die,
" Which GOD's own Fountain does fupply."

EPI-

EPIGRAM.

WITH folded Hands and lifted Eyes,
    "Have Mercy, Heav'n," the Parson
       cries;
"And on our Sun-burnt, thirsty Plains,
"Thy Blessings send in genial Rains."
The Sermon ended, and the Pray'rs,
The Parson to be gone prepares;
When with a Look, brighten'd in Smiles,
"Thank Heav'n! it rains," cries Farmer *Giles*:
"Rains!" quo' the Parson---"Sure you Joke;
"Rains!—*Heav'n forbid---I han't my Cloak!*"

The

The D O V E S.

I.

TWO fonder Turtles never woo'd
 On Hill or fhady Grove;
In murm'ring Notes they bill'd, they coo'd,
 And anfwer'd *Love for Love.*

II.

Their little Bofoms thought no Ill,
 The Murd'rer ey'd his Game;
He heard 'em coo---He faw 'em bill,
 Yet---took his fatal Aim:

III.

He fir'd;——he fhed the trueft Blood
 E'er warm'd a Turtle's Heart;
Amaz'd *Colombo's* Partner ftood,
 Nor from his Side wou'd part.

IV.

" If, Murd'rer, thou *canft* Mercy fhow,
 " Here aim your welcome Stroke;
" Again, again repeat your Blow;
 " Your Vengeance I invoke."

He

V.

He levell'd, and his Aim was true;
  She *wiſh'd* the fatal Shot;
The Piece recoil'd; it burſt, it flew
  The Murd'rer on the Spot.

VI.

'Twas *Venus'* Work:---Her vengeful Hand,
  To Death the Savage dooms:------
She ſpeaks---and at her high Command,
  Colombo Life reſumes.

VII.

Grateful, their warmeſt Thanks they pay,
  To the bright Queen of Love;
Who, watchful of their amorous Play,
  Ev'n wiſh'd herſelf a Dove.

VIII.

Their little Hearts with Bliſs o'er-ran,
  Strait to the Grove they flew;
And to the Haunts of murd'rous Man,
  Murmur'd a long *Adieu.*

To

To Mr —— Y———, on his Marriage with a most joyous Lady.

THO! fome talk of your Marriage queerly,
I wifh you Joy, *Tom*, moft fincerely ;
And Joy that Hufband muft poffefs,
Whofe Wife's the Source of *Joyoufnefs* :
Whofe Wife has Hundreds happy made,
Quite Miftrefs of the *joycus* Trade ;
What endlefs Joys to him are known,
Who all thofe Joys now calls his own ;
Too much for one poor Man to bear,
With Friends you'll therefore kindly fhare.

I hope, dear *Tom*, you've now for Life
Got a moft *joyous*, active Wife ;
To whom both *Will* and *Pow'r* are given,
Of making Spoufy free of Heaven ;
And who—(*Can* Love be more expreft ?)
Wou'd damn herfelf to make You bleft.

Your Friends all wifh you Joy, and hope
You've now of Joy---a *Cornu-Cope* :---
One *Cornu-Cope* perhaps won't do ;
Why then, dear *Tom*, We wifh you *Two*.

An

An EPILOGUE.

ACTORS are grown religious now-a-days,
And Epilogues are Graces after Plays:
I hope our *Opera* prov'd a decent Treat,
And Grace, you know, fhou'd follow after Meat.

Quite tir'd with Singing, cou'd I but prevail,
Inftead of Epilogue, you'd hear a Tale?---
Thank ye, I read your Looks; content they feem;
A Tale I'll give, and Mufic be my Theme.

Springing from Earth, a Lark had new begun
To hail with Mattins the uprifing Sun,
When a huge Boar, juft tumbling from his Sty,
Thus grunted to the Warbler of the Sky:
" Zoons! what a hideous Noife! that fcreaming
              " Note!
" I wifh Old *Nick* was dancing down your Throat;
" You fee me wallow quiet in my Dung,
" I eat my Puddings, and I hold my Tongue:
" Why can't you live like me?--Cram and be wife;
" In cramming---ugh!---the greateft Pleafure lies.

The Lark his Mufic for a Moment ceas'd,
And thus addrefs'd the long-ear'd, grunting Beaft:
" Peace, growling Wretch! unfeeling of thofe
              " Joys,
" Which Thou and Savages like Thee call Noife:
                        " Thought-

" Thoughtlefs of Earth, I warbling upward rove,
" Tow'rds Heav'n, the Seat of Mufic and of Love:
" Or if, perchance, my Eyes to Earth I bend,
" My Carrols for a Moment I fufpend;
" Pitying, I view the *half-enliven'd* Throng,
" To *Mufic* callous, and the thrilling Song:
" 'Tis a fixth Senfe, by kind indulgent Heaven
" To favour'd Man and feather'd Songfters given:
" Where Mufic's felt, we tafte the Blifs of Gods;
" Without it, Larks, like Boars, were breathing
              " Clods:
" Rowl in your Filth; grunt on---nor dare decry
" Beings fuperior---Tenants of the Sky."

So faid, the little Warbler upwards fprung,
And left the carping Boar in Filth and Dung;
While the grofs Savage, from his kindred Mud
Stood gaping, nor one Warble underftood:

Tho' Boars, fometimes, the Human Form
      difgrace,
Such, never yet, thank Heaven, were feen within
      this Place.

An

An E P I L O G U E,
Spoken by Mrs ———, after playing the Character of
Lady B R U T E.

As Criminal on Gibbet high fufpended,
A dreadful warning Piece to All's intended,
Juft fo---Poor Lady *Brute*'s unhappy Fate
Seems to proclaim---*Beware the married State.*

But judge not, Ladies, that a wedded Life
Is a perpetual Fund of Hate and Strife ;
When *Hymen* fmiles, his Joys are next divine,
Friendfhip and Love their fweeteft Flowers entwine :
Believe me,---for of both I've ftood the Teft,
A fingle Life is but *Half* Life at beft.

Some Sir *John Brutes*, I own, are to be found,
But, Heav'n be prais'd, thofe Monfters don't abound :
Yet when to fuch in Wedlock we are given,
Are we not kind to fend the *Brutes* to Heaven ?

Search the World thro', in general you'll find,
That Marriage is a Draught of the *mix'd* Kind,
A Cordial bitter-fweet, a pleafing Pain ;
An *April*-Day, now Sun-fhine and now Rain ;
A League *Defenfive*---and---alas, too true---
It (fometimes) proves a League *Offenfive* too :
'Tis, in the Jockey's Phrafe, a *Give-and-Take*,
Where each fome fmall Allowances fhou'd make.

The

The Marrimonial Tree all Taſtes can ſuit;
It yields at once both ſweet and acid Fruit:
The Sweet--too luſcious, oftimes is amended,
When with a little Daſh of Acid blended:
And ſure the Acid were a ſad Repaſt,
Did not the blended Sweet correct the Taſte:
With genuine Spirits mix'd in *Hymen*'s Bowl,
A pleaſing Draught they make to glad the Soul.

But oh, this Caution let me beg you'd take,—
Be ſparing of the Acid for Love's Sake;
A *little* Acid gives a pleaſing Zeſt,
But *Much*—the Cholic breeds, and don't digeſt.

From Sir *John*'s Fate learn, Huſbands, to be
            wiſe;
Govern you may, but ne'er ſhou'd tyrannize;
If you wou'd have Us *Honour and Obey*,
To *Love and Cheriſh* is your wiſeſt Way.

EPITAPHS.

Designed for a Favourite Actor.

FAREWELL Horror, Rage, and Love,
 Farewell all the Soul can move;
Farewell Humour, Wit, and Joke,
Here *Nature's Looking-Glass* lies broke.

On a young Gentleman who died of Love.

HERE rests whom Fortune and the Muses
   blest,
Of Wealth, Good-nature, Learning, Wit poffeft;
Happy he rov'd, and was the blytheft Swain,
That ever tun'd his Pipes on *Scotia's* Plain;
'Till Love, malicious, aim'd a fatal Dart,
And, maugre Virtue's Shield, transfix'd his Heart;
Haplefs, he faw his Love gave *Stella* Pain,
To give her Eafe—his Heart's Core burft in twain.

Q   IT

IT matters not who sleeps within this Tomb,
To this same Resting Place *You* soon must
come ;
This is the Journey's End of Great and Small,
We all must take a Lodging in *Worm-Hall.*

✕✕✕✕✕✕✕✕✕✕✕✕✕✕✕✕✕✕✕✕✕✕✕✕

On a Welshman.

LET None dare approach who in Birth
are deficient ;
A *Welshman* lies here——that is Reason sufficient

On ————

WITH Safety *Truth* may now appear ;
Her greatest Foe lies bury'd here.

On an Honest Poor Farmer.

LET not the Great indulge a scornful Frown,
When told——" Here lies, what *was,* an
honest Clown :"
Tho' humble, yet his Pride was often seen ;
He scorn'd, tho' low, to stoop to what was mean :
To Virtue if Reward above be given,
This *Clown* on Earth, *Ennobled* is in Heaven.

On

On Mrs ————

THE Heart that felt for other's Woe,
   That warm'd with Virtue's sacred Glow,
Is *Cold—Clay-cold*:—No more her Eyes
Virtue's pure Fount with Tears supplies:
All *Cold* and silent too that Tongue
Where soft Persuasion ever hung:
Those Lips, where Sweetness still repos'd,
Truth's Portals,—now are ever clos'd:
The Mother!-----may to bless Mankind,
Children unborn such Mothers find!---
The tender Wife!---but Words are weak;
The Husband's Tears her Worth must speak——
Here lies:——
Be humble, Mortals, learn your Doom,
To this *Cold* Bed we all must come:
Since *Virtue's* Favourite lies here,
'Twere Virtue now to shed a Tear.

❀❀❀❀❀❀❀❀❀❀❀❀❀❀❀❀❀❀❀❀❀❀❀❀❀❀❀❀

Written over a Burial Vault.

ONE common Boast attends King, Clown,
    and Hero,
Contain'd in this few Words——*Sum, Fui, Ero.*

EPI-

EPIGRAMS, &c.

IF *Wilkes*'s Schemes they mean to blaſt,
    And ſtop his bold Career;
They muſt forgive him all that's paſt,
    And make him a *Scotch* PEER.

Scriblerius.

On the Downfall of the Jeſuits.

YE Sophiſts train'd up in *Ignatius*' College,
    For Shame! what's become of your Wiſdom
        and Knowledge?
'Tis gone—And we find that the Axiom is true,
Si itis Jeſuitis———non itis Jeſu.

Quiblerius.

TO pleaſe *Pygmalion*, Heav'n inſpir'd with
        Life
A Tongueleſs Stone, of which he made a Wife;
Wou'd Heav'n, all-gracious, hear *Aſino*'s Moan,
His Wife----her Tongue at leaſt----wou'd ſoon
    be Stone.

On

On a Physician and Man-Midwife.

PHYSICIAN and Man-Mdwife join'd in
   One!
Both Life and Death his Pow'r unbounded own;
This Hand to Life inducts us from the Womb;
The other gives us, Pill-ftruck, to the Tomb.

FROM feafting on *Garrick* how often we find
 Fools feaft upon *Harlequin*, more to their
   Mind!
Thus Flies, 'tis obferv'd, from a Tafte as abfurd,
On Honey firft *feed*;————then————*indulge* on
  a T—d.

On an eminent Actor.

WHILE Fools in *Bufo* think they fee
  The True *Vis Comica* expreft;
Your Men of Judgement all agree,
  'Tis meer *Phiz Comica* at beft.

On another of the same Profession.

TO touch our Hearts nor fighs nor Tears
    neglected;
You'll ne'er *affect:*——The Reafon?——You're
    affected.

* *

CRIES *Gnatho*----" In *Ireland* what Plenty
    " were found,
" Were your Bogs but well drain'd, and trans-
    " form'd to dry Ground:"
" No, no, (with a Sigh replies *Dermot*) 'tis
    " plain,
" Poor *Ireland* too much, by St *Patrick*, they
    " drain."

* *

THE Difference you afk me, *Jack,*
    'Twixt *Mævius* and Dean *Swift;*
The one of Writing has the *Knack;*
    The other has the *Gift.*.

S.

On

On seeing the Picture of Justice over the Judge's Seat.

WHILE *P--e*, with Brow fevere, and
    formal Saw,
From the Learn'd Bench expounds the Myftic Law;
See *Juftice* o'er his Head as Symbol ftand,
The Sword and well-pois'd Scale in either Hand;
But *P--e*, to prove the Goddefs a meer Farce,
Unmanner'd Brute!---Towards her turns his A-fe.

※ ※ ※ ※ ※ ※ ※ ※ ※

A *Yorkfhire* 'Squire, with Looks that fneer'd
    forth Scorn,
Cries,----" Prithee, Honeft Friend, where were
    you born?"——
" In *Ireland*, faith," cries *Patrick*:——" Nor
    would I,
" Ev'n tho'. in *Yorkfhire* born, the Truth deny."

" YOU

" YOU keep your Poſt Chariot, dear *Galen*,
" I ſee ;"——
" You miſtake, my dear Friend, my Poſt Chariot
" keeps me."

WHILE *Stentor* in *Dumont* appears,
    And, ſighing, pours forth Floods of Tears;
How ſtrangely various People's Whim!
He weeps;---Spectators laugh at Him:
Tho' diff'rent, juſt is their Deciſion;
Rowe merits Tears, *Stentor* Deriſion.

" A Hearty Drubbing, *Will*, you know,
"   For your damn'd Negligence I owe :"
" Good Sir, for Trifles never fret,"
Cries *Will*---" For, *I forgive the Debt.*"

R U F A

*R*UFA Advances makes;---What can she do?
Virgins of Thirty-fix are *forc'd* to woo:---
Yet droop not, *Rufa*, I have known some Men,
To a young Chick prefer a tough old Hen;
If so, who knows what still thy Fate may be,
Some Fool may chance to stick his Fork in thee.

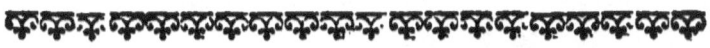

*On Reading in the Newspapers of the Marriage of a
young Lady, whose least Accomplishment was
said to be* 2000 *l. a Year.*

*C*LOE's Two Thousand Pound a Year,
Her least Accomplishment's we hear;
Her *least* Accomplishment !---'Tis true---
But then it is her *Greatest too.*

*T*HE Man who on his Wit depends,
Can seldom boast great Store of Friends;
And he who to himself is wise,
Not on his *Wit*—but *Wits* relies.

What

What is it Like?

HUMOUR and fportive Mirth abound,
And—*What's Love like?*—goes laughing
    round;
Quo' *Hall,* " Love's like a Tragedy,
" Where Death's the fure Cataftrophe :"
Cries *Senex*---" Love, I think, is fcarce
" Superior to a One Act Farce :"
" I rather think," replete with Glee,
Cries *Nan,* " that Love's a Comedy,
" Where every Act, tho' full of Sport,
" In my Opinion is too fhort ;
" So tedious too each Interlude,
" We long to have the Play renew'd."

IF Wit be what your Wits have faid in Mirth,
" A quick Conception, and an eafy Birth,"
No more their feeble Claim let Men avow,
Wit's fprightly Wreathe muft grace the Female
    Brow.

Man

Man Refined.

ADAM we're told was form'd of plaſtic Earth,
 And Eve to Clay-ſprung Adam ow'd her Birth;
As much ſuperior Adam we ſuppoſe
To the dull lifeleſs Clod from whence he roſe,
So much at leaſt ſuperior we conceive
To Clay-ſprung Adam was his Rib-ſprung Eve.

※※※※※※※※※※※※

'TIS an Axiom well known, deny it who can,
 That a Taylor is but the ninth Part of a
  Man;
'Tis an Axiom approv'd too, that each jolly Tar,
Makes nine common Men, or in Peace or in War:
Theſe Truths once premis'd-----'Tis plain that
  Two Sailors
Make more than one Hundred and Sixty Poor
  Taylors.

On two beautiful Female Friends.

FAIR *Phillis* and *Cloe* are never afunder,
   The *Wonderful Beauty*, and *beautiful Wonder*;
Such *wonderful* Beauties thofe Beauties can boaft,
We *wond'ring* behold, and in *Wonder* are loft;
And where Two fuch *Wonders* againft us confpire,
No *Wonder* the World fhould in *Wonder* expire.

PETER WONDERFUL.

To Live Well.

IF He who is *Good* may be faid to *Live well*,
   And if to *Live well* be to *Keep a good Table*;
Then he who *eats beft* muft in *Goodnefs* excell,
And *Virtue* and *Vice* are no more than a *Fable*.

On *VOLTAIRE*.

ENTHUSIASTS, Lutherans, and Monks,
  Jews, Syndics, Calvinists, and Punks,
    Voltaire an Atheist call;
While he, unhurt, in placid Mood,
To prove himself a Christian good,
    Kindly forgives them all.

GOOD *Bavius* each Day at the Chapel is
        seen,
And Saint-like declaims at Romances obscene;
Yet *Bavius* can read, when he's snugly alone,
The Woman of Pleasure, with *Spectacles* on.

On *seeing the Interlude of* Neptune *and* Amphitrite, *in* Shakespeare's Tempest, *performed.*

WHILE Ocean's Deity and Pride,
  O'er *Amphitrite*, his fair Bride,
Enamour'd hangs,—her milky Chest
And heaving Globes his Eyes arrest:
Fidelia, with a smiling Look,
That Archness and Good-nature spoke,
Thus cries ——— ———
  " Or I'm mistaken, or the Dish,
  " *Neptune* admires,——is *Flesh*, not *Fish*."

R   On

On Two remarkable Orators, who exhibited Lectures of Elocution alternately the same Night, at ——— Theatre.

WHILE *Fatuus* like a Madman rants
      and raves,
And sleeping Spectres rouses from their Graves ;
Crassus, with dull, unvaried, Nurse-like Strain,
Most kindly *Lullabies* them back again.

CLEORA's Breasts two Hillocks are of Snow,
  On which Two little fragrant Rose-Buds grow;
Between those Hills lies *Cupid*'s Down-smooth
      Vale,
Where *Jove* himself enraptur'd might regale,
And lodg'd within, a treasur'd Heart is known,
Form'd like her Sister *Medicis*—of *Stone*.

On reading Mrs Macauley's History of the Stewarts.

TO shame the Luke-warm Patriots of the Age,
  And wake 'em to a genuine British Rage,
See, *Liberty* herself from Heav'n appears,
And fair *Macauley*'s Form the Goddess wears.

The

The MERCIFUL.

A Butcher with a Heart as hard as Stone,
 And callous to an Orphan Lambkin's Moan,
Seizes his fated Prey with horrid Grin,
And whistles while the Knife he plunges in;
Nell, who the Scene beheld, with piteous Looks,
And shrugg'd-up Shoulders, thus her Feelings
   spoke:
" The barb'rous Wretch! thus, unprovok'd,
   " to spill
" The Blood of a poor Lamb that ne'er did Ill!—
" See, how the little Creature pants for Life,
" The Murd'rer's Jaws clasping the reeky Knife:
" To do a Deed like this, were I to gain
" The Universe—ev'n such a Bribe were vain."
Thus *Nell* with Tenderness exclaims and feels——
While all the Time——good Soul!——*She skins*
  live Eels.

On seeing. Miss ——— bathing in the Sea.

IN Pity to the Torments that I feel,
Transform your Votary, *Venus*, to an Eel;
In that wish'd Form, I'd stroll yon liquid Space,
And find, by Instinct led, a resting Place,
A snug Retreat, the Lover's fav'rite Prize,
Where, with Love's Tide, I safe might fall
          and rise;
There, with extatic Joys, I'd glad expire,
Unquench'd by *Neptune*, in Love's heav'nly Fire.

A R I D D L E.

IN Battle the Stoutest—Nor is it a Wonder—
To this strange *Phænomenon* always strike under:
Ne marle like a Monster in Fight shou'd prevail,
Whose Head (Lord preserve us) lies hid in its Tail.

A PASTORAL.

THE Sun juſt peeping o'er the Hills was ſeen,
 The Birds all caroll'd, and the Air was
   ſheen;
Garlands, of Daffodils and Tulips made,
With Cowſlips, gathered from the unforc'd Glade,
O'er ev'ry Cottage Door, in Trim ſo gay,
Spoke a glad Welcome to the wiſh'd-for *May:*
Dight in their gayeſt Cloaths, each Shepherd
   Swain
And Village Nymph trip'd o'er the green-ſwerd
   Plain;
While *Cupid* made ſuch Havock among Hearts,
His full-ſtor'd Quiver ſcarce ſupply'd him Darts:
In ev'ry Breaſt Joy revell'd this glad Morn,
Save *Deborah*'s:—She, hapleſs Maid, forlorn,
With Eyes brimful, beneath a Yew reclin'd
Sat,—dulling with her Sighs the paſſing Wind;
When *Margery*, light tripping o'er the Graſs,
Stopp'd ſhort, and (wond'ring) thus accoſts
   the Laſs.

MARGERY.

Am I awake? Is't *Deborah* I ſee
With blubber'd Cheeks?—Quite loſt her wonted
   Glee?
What, *Deb?*—That erſt ſo frolickſome was ſeen;
The blytheſt Maid that danc'd upon the Green!

Up, up, for Shame, nor longer dowley fret,
Around the Pole the Lads and Girls are met;
Blind *Giles* his Fiddle fcrapes in Notes fo fweet,
You'd think, for fure, he witch'd their Puppet
     Feet:
Have you forgot this is the Firft of *May?*
When dight in their new Robes the Fields look
     gay:
On ev'ry Hedge the fcent;d Bloffoms fpring,
The Birds their fweeteft Carrols joyous fing;
The Cuckow, dumb 'till now, this Morn effays,
In mellow Notes his Summer Song to raife:
Up, up, for Shame, and to the Sports repair;
Our Sweethearts both, believe me, Girl, are *there:*
Whence comes this Change?——What fad Mis-
     fortune, fay,——
Can caufe thofe Tears, and Looks of wild Difmay?

DEBORAH.

Ah, haplefs Maid!——when you my Griefs
     fhall hear,
Too foon, alas, you'll anfwer Tear for Tear;
Tummas, the Lad to whom I gave my Heart,
Tummas and I for ay muft henceforth part;
He and thy Sweetheart, *Hodge*, both lifted are,
And now to fight with *Frenchmen* muft prepare.

         M. A R.

MARGERY.

You fright me, *Deborah*;—nay, deareſt Maid,
Was it in Joke or Earneſt what you ſaid?

DEBORAH.

Too true I wiſs the News—for Farmer *John*
Saw the Lads ſtrutting with their red Coats on;
Laſt Night the Serjeant, with his Copper Lace,
(Woe worth his oily Tongue and brazen Face)
Entic'd 'em to the *Royal Oak*—and there,
Firſt made 'em drunk—and then—they liſted were.

MARGERY.

My *Roger* Liſted! *Margery*'s undone,
With *Roger* every Joy and Comfort's flown;
Was it for this ſuch ſugar'd Words you ſpoke,
When the bent Six pence lovingly we broke?—
Was it for this I've oftimes been foretold,
That bleſt with *Roger*'s Love I ſhould grow old?
Nor *Sieve* or *Sheers* I'll henceforth e'er believe,
Nor ſhall St *Agnes*'s Faſt again deceive;
Nor credit more a Six-pence put in *Ruth*,*
(Strange! that the Bible thus ſhould tell Untruth!)

For

---

* 'Tis a Cuſtom among Country Girls to put the Bible
under their Pillows at Night, with Six-pence clapt in the
Book of *Ruth*; in order to dream of the Man deſtined to be
their Huſbands.

For all my Hopes—Woe's me!—are overblown,
Since Sweetheart *Roger* for a Soldier's gone.

DEBORAH.

The Bride-cake which I got when Farmer
    Hale
Married the buxom Widow of the Dale,
Beneath my Bolſter plac'd in Kerchief white,
I dreamt of Nought but *Tummas* all the Night:
I thought—but *Margery*, you oft have known,
And well my Dreams may gueſs at by your own:—
Nor Dreams or Bride-cake henceforth I'll believe,
For Dreams and Bride-cake both alike deceive.

MARGERY.

The Dew, which I this Morn with ſo much
    Care
Gather'd from yon green Field to make me fair,
I'll fling away—Nor henchforth, well I ween,
This blubber'd Face, ought elſe, ſave Tears,
        ſhall clean;
For what avails a comely Face to boaſt,
Since all I prize, ah me! in *Roger*'s loſt.

DEBORAH.

When *Tummas* cut his Hand—upon the Wound,
To ſtop the Blood, a Cob-web ſtrait I bound;
Next Day he told me I had heal'd the Smart,
And, ſmiling, wiſh'd me heal his bleeding Heart;

I

I blufh'd—he kifs'd me;—and with fugar'd Words,
And Tongue, as foft and fmooth as unbroke
    Curds,
He made me plight my Troth; and on a Book
Swear to be his: The Oath we jointly took:
He fwore my *True Love* he would live and die;—
Are Lovers True,—who from their *True Loves* fly?

MARGERY.

Laft *April*-tide—(I little thought fo foon,
Laft *April*-tide, to part with my dear Loon)
Like *Roger* none fuch matchlefs Wit cou'd fhow,
Or make fo many *April* Fools, I trow.

DEBORAH.

A few Days gone, (how tender *Tummas'* Breaft!)
From a rude Lad he fav'd a Linnet's Neft;
He fwore, and fwore aloud,—It was a Shame
To murder Birds of any Sort but *Game:*
How can a Heart, fo tender and fo good,
Then make a Trade of fhedding Chriftian Blood?

MARGERY.

In Wreftling no one Lad can *Hodge* excell;
At Cudgels too he always bore the Bell;
And but laft Wake, when a rude Fellow fwore
He'd have a Kifs, and my lac'd Kerchief tore,
I fcream'd:—*Hodge* flew like Lightning to my Aid,
And at his Feet the Brute was quickly laid.

DEBO-

DEBORAH.

In Dancing, who with *Tummas* cou'd compare?
Or foot it on the Green with such an Air?
At Church too none so loud the Psalms cou'd sing;
He shak'd and quaver'd so, he made all ring:
And then to hear him chaunt Bold *Robin Hood*,
Or *Marg'ret*'s grimly Ghost, what Hours I've
    stood !——
I cou'd not stir—I was all Ears and Eyes;
Dame might scold on;—I told her twenty Lies:——
And when he whistled, *Margery*, I swear,
Nor Flutes nor Black-birds cou'd with him
    compare.

MARGERY.

A Swallow's Nest, which for five Summers stood,
The Nursery of many a callow Brood,
Just o'er my Casement;—where the Jessamine
And Honey-Suckle rival Sweets entwine;
(Where Swallows build, good Fortune still is
    known)
Last Easter Day,——Woe's me!——came
    tumbling down:
The Bird return'd from foreign Parts yestreen,
And seem'd to pass the Spot, and mourn, I ween,
And now its Nest builds elsewhere—as if struck,
My Window was the Dwelling of Ill-Luck.

DEBO-

DEBORAH.

The other Night—to think on't makes me weep,
When Cocks, Hens, Pigs, and Christians were
    asleep;
Into our Barn the crafty *Reynard* stole,
He made his Way thro' yonder tiny Hole;
The Hens, all flutt'ring, with a piteous Cry
Proclaim'd aloud the murd'rous Fox was nigh;
Wak'd with the Noise, I started in my Smock,
And scream'd aloud———" My Cock? My
    " Ginger Cock!"
I came too late—my Ginger Cock was gone;——
" My Cock!" I cry'd—and fell into a Swoon:
Crafty the Fox; the Serjeant craftier far,
Who in his Clutches thus can *Tummas* bear:
Another *Ginger* I may get again,
But never, never get so sweet a Swain.

MARGERY.

No more shall Bees to flowery Meads resort,
Nor with their willing Mates Cock-Sparrows
    sport;
No more in the *Red-Sea* Goblins be laid,
Or Midnight Fairies pinch the slattern Maid;
The Gipsy's Hand no more shall Maidens cross,
Or more the Coffee-Dish shall trembling toss,
The Lambs shall cease to bleat, the Cocks to crow,
When Tears for my poor *Roger* cease to flow.

DEBO-

DEBORAH.

Sooner the heavy Ox ſhall flit thro' Air,
Sooner with Turtles rav'nous Kites ſhall pair;
The Hogs ſhall ſing in ſoft melodious Notes,
And Nightingales ſhall, gruntling, ſtretch their
Throats ;
Sooner the 'Squire his Rent when due refuſe,
Or ſmalleſt Sheaves, in Tything, Parſons chuſe;
Sooner than—Break thou ſtubborn Heart, in twain,
Sleeping or waking I forget my Swain.

Thus waild the Maids, when on the Plain
appear'd
Tummas and *Roger*, whom the 'Squire had clear'd,
The welcome Sight at once diſpell'd their Fears,
Kiſſes and *May*-day Fare dried up their Tears,
The Swains their Wiſhes had, the longing
Maidens theirs.

The LION and WASP.

A FABLE.

A Lion, whose Blood-thirsty Reign
  Bespoke him *Nero* of the Plain;
Who judg'd that the sole End of Power
Was to destroy and to devour;
Who knew no Law but Tyrant Will,
Still prompt to ravage, fleece, and kill,
Thus proudly roars—" With *Jove* I vie,
" I rule the Earth, he rules the Sky;
" His Thunder makes the Heavens quake,
" My Roaring makes the Forests shake;
" Death ever waits my Kingly Sway,
" While four-legg'd crouching Slaves obey;
" They breathe but by my Courtesy,
" And the whole World was made for Me:—
" *Britannia*'s Monarch I disdain,
" Who rules by Love a willing Plain;
" Like fam'd *Morocco*'s Prince I move,
" By Fear I govern, not by Love.

Thus vaunts the *Grand Monarque*: Around
His servile Courtiers lick the Ground,
When with a careless Air and Grace,
A buzzing Wasp flies near the Place,

S Skims

Skims thro' the Air, nor bends the Wing
In Homage to the mighty King;——
Which fo incens'd his Majefty,
That with his Tail erected high,
He ftrikes the Infect to the Earth,
And fpoils his Mufic and his Mirth.——
" Shall a mean worthlefs Infect dare
" Unbidden in our Sight appear?
" When Infolence thus dare prefume,
" Death---certain Death fhall be its Doom."

Tho' ftunn'd at firft---with venom'd Spite,
The Wafp foon wings his circling Flight;
He vows Revenge, and on his Foe,
With Sting erect he aims the Blow:
" Tyrant (he cries) what cou'd provoke
" Without a Caufe thy barb'rous Stroke?
" From Want of Food can it proceed?
" Lions on Infects never feed:
" The Reafon's plain, thy cruel Breaft
" Is with a human Soul poffeft;
" 'Twas Wantonnefs provok'd the Deed,
" To pleafe your Pride, ev'n Wafps muft bleed:
" But, Tyrant, take before I die
" An injur'd Wafp's laft Legacy:"
So faid, he darts with rapid Wing
The Noftrils of the fhaggy King,
To the extremeft Verge afcends,
There all his wafpifh Venom fpends;

And

And near the Brain's monaſtic Cell
He pours his macerating Spell:——
The Tyrant roars, and o'er the Plain,
He drives, in all the Hell of Pain;
The Foreſts tremble with his Cries,
Quick to his Brain the Venom flies,
And raging mad, he tears, blaſphemes, and dies. }

Thus Bubble Pride and Cruelty,
 Thoſe pageant Tyrants of an Hour,
Are often forc'd to bend the Knee,
 Ev'n to a paltry Inſect's Power.

The

The TRIPLE ALLIANCE.

AS *Phœbus* feated on high *Pindus* Brow,
Beam'd forth his Bleſſings on the World
below ;
While round his Throne the tuneful Siſters play,
And *Wit* and *Muſic* hail the God of Day,
Folly with grinning Face, and vacant Head,
And *Vice*, to Joy and Feeling ever dead,
With black *Hypocriſy*, their favourite Child,
(By ſome the *Spleen*, ſome *Superſtition* ſtil'd)
Cringing approach'd the Throne, and thus they
ſpoke :——
" Your Juſtice, mighty *Phœbus*, we invoke;
" Shall *Satyr*, *Wit*, and *Humour*,——thoſe low
" Things,
" Who can't like Us a Lineage boaſt from Kings
" Shall *They* from the curſt Stage their Ar-
" rows ſend,
" And True *Religion* impiouſly offend ?
" Say is it fitting *We* ſhould bend the Knee
" And dread *Thalia* and *Melpomene?*
" The Stage deſtroy'd, we ſhou'd no more
" complain,
" But Mankind own our Univerſal Reign."

With Brow contraſted, and diſdainful Eye,
Melpomene advanc'd to make reply,
When

When with a fprightly Archnefs in her Look,
Thalia thus the kindred Pefts befpoke;
" Sweet Madam *Vice*, from whom we pluck the
" Veil,
" And fhew the World what you wou'd fain
" conceal;
" And Goodman *Folly*, whofe chaotic Rule,
" Mankind would own, but for my Ridicule;
" And Thou, *Hypocrify*, of Senfe the Shame,
" Who impioufly ufurp'ft *Religion*'s Name,
" Tho' differing wide, as *Guinea*'s footy Train,
" From thofe fair Nymphs who grace *Britan-*
" *nia*'s Plain;
" The Mufes' Looking-Glafs fhall fhow ye bare,
" Not as Ye *wou'd* appear, but as Ye *are*;
" Stript of Difguife, your Souls we will difplay,
" And hunt ye as the wildeft Beafts of Prey;
" And tho', while Men have Paffions, fo fays
" Fate,
" We can't a certain, lafting Cure create,
" We'll ftill, with Virtue's Aid, your Pow'r affail,
" And make ye feel the Force of *Tickle-Tail*."

So faid, her Lafh fhe rear'd, and at the Sight,
The Fiends, trembling with Rage and venom'd
Spite,
Vanifh'd, *like* Fiends, conceal'd in Shades of
Night.

Let

Let bloated *Envy* gnaw the bloody File,
The *Mufes* and their *Priefls* at *Envy* fmile;
Unwounded ftill the Inftrument remains,
'Tis *Envy*'s Blood the crimfon'd File diftains.

On

" MAY Heaven this Boon in Mercy grant,
"   'Tis all I wifh, 'tis all I want;
" A youthful Bride to grace my Bed,
" In Honour's ftricteft Precepts bred;
" Sweet-temper'd, gentle as a Dove,
" 'Till now an Alien to Love;
" With Beauty to direct the Dart,
" And Virtue to fecure my Heart;
" Above Coquetting; bleft with Senfe;
" Whofe ev'ry Look is Eloquence;
" Fiom Pride and Scandal ever free,
" And from difguftful Prudery:
" In Habit neat, in Perfon clean,
" A Stranger to corroding Spleen;
" A Voice to charm my Soul to Reft,
" Whene'er by worldly Cares oppreft;
" No fiery Zealot in Religion,
" A Soul defpifing Superftition;
" Whofe Senfe directs her how to blend
" The Wife, the Lover, and the Friend:—
" In ev'ry Shape above Difguife,
" Her Soul depictur'd in her Eyes;
" A Fortune eafy and fecure,
" Tho' that fhou'd be my fmalleft Lure:——
                 " Ent'ring

" Ent'ring my Doors, I'd have her meet me
" With Smiles,——and ſtill with Welcomes
" greet me :—
" Wou'd *Jove* in Pity hear my Pray'r,
" And bleſs my Days with ſuch a Fair,
" I'd never quit ſo rich a Treaſure,
" To roam abroad in Search of Pleaſure;
" But uſe my ev'ry Pow'r and Art,
" To win, and to preſerve her Heart."

Thus *D—* pray'd; and Father *Jove*
Heard ev'ry Syllable above.

Quo' *Jove*—" A modeſt, droll *quelque Choſe,*
" He'll nought for Want of aſking loſe;
" Suppoſe for once the Whim I try,
" And with the Youth's Addreſs comply;
" He's been a looſe young Spark, I'm ſure,
" Who knows but this may work a Cure;
" He don't want Senſe; he may amend;
" 'Tis a long Lane that knows no End:
" Here, *Hymen,* take your Torch and fly,
" Quick, in the Twinkling of an Eye,
" Fly to Miſs *E——,* of *Y--k,*
" You'll find her buſy at her Work;
" She don't, like other Ladies, kill
" Her Time in Scandal or Quadrille,
" Or reading paltry, dull Romances,
" To fill her Brain with fooliſh Fancies;
" Tho'

" Tho' full of Cheerfulnefs and Spirit,
" She fcorns to mifemploy her Merit;
" In ufeful Sort her Hours fhe fpends,
" In working, chatting with her Friends,
" Or reading, where fhe's fure to find,
" A Banquet worthy of her Mind;
" In walking, or at Church in Pray'r,
" (She's not afham'd of going there)
" Prefent her as a Gift from *Jove*;
" And you, my little God of *Love*,
" Juft at the Inftant take him flap—
" As you know how—beneath Left Pap,
" And on the Fair, with twanging Bow,
" The felf-fame Compliment beftow :——
" But fhould the Youth ungrateful prove,
" And ceafe to, *Cherifh* and to *Love*,
" Tell him—With Punifhments I'll teaze him,
" A thoufand Pains and Achs fhall feize him;
" And *in Terrorem* to bad Spoufes,
" I'll burn his Pictures, Books, and Houfes;
" Nay, worfe than all—the Bleffing giv'n,
" I'll re-affume, and fnatch to Heav'n :——
" But hold, I'm rather too fevere,
" To threaten thus, 'ere Faults appear;
" For Gratitude, with Senfe and Truth,
" Have ever harbour'd in the Youth;
" And Honour, Cement to the whole,
" Is rooted in his inmoft Soul :———

" Tell

" Tell him, in fhort, he may depend
" On *Jove*—if Conftant—as his Friend."

The Meffage giv'n—Quick from the Sky
To *Y--k* the winged Couriers fly;
And to the wifhing Youth convey
The yielding Maid (like fragrant *May*
Blufhing, when doom'd her glowing Charms
To her belov'd *Zephyrus*' Arms)
Kneeling, the Bleffing he receives,
And fcarce his ravifh'd Sight believes :——
Cupid, fly Rogue!---with barbed Darts,
Transfixes both the Lovers' Hearts;
The *Gordian* Knot while *Hymen* frames,
His Torch ne'er fent forth brighter Flames;
Nor has it fince been trimm'd, they fay,
But burns ftill brighter ev'ry Day;
And *Jove* upon his Honour fwears,
(I mean, 'pon Honour he declares)
He ne'er a happier Couple knew,
More kind,---more loving,---and more true.

DELICACY.

FALSE *Delicacy*, Poppy-crown'd and chaste,
  Meer Water-Gruel, flat and void of Taste;
A Rainbow Being, nourish'd long in *France*,
Her Parents *Affectation* and *Romance*;
A Sentimental Miss, so wond'rous good,
She scorns, or seems to scorn, meer Flesh and Blood;
With Looks demure, and prim as antique Maid,
When all her wou'd-be Virtues are display'd;
To cheerful Wit and Humour Foe profest,
(Humour and Wit your Buckram Prudes detest)
If the insipid Trifler you wou'd know,
Our modern Comedies the Nothing show;
In Novels chief the flimsey Shadow reigns,
By Nymphs   ador'd,   and eke by Nymph-like
                  Swains.

  Not so *True Delicacy*, heav'nly Fair,
Whose Parents smiling *Truth* and *Nature* are,
To Virtue's tend'rest Feelings tho' inclin'd,
Yet unreserv'd, and of a cheerful Mind;
Tho' chaste, yet free---tho' humble, never mean,
A Foe to Pride, to Prudery, and the Spleen;
Aided by her, Nature a Polish takes,
And genial Fancy every happy wakes;
Open to Pleasure, oft is seen to smile,
Nor thinks *bon Mots*, tho' *Janus*-fac'd, defile;
                                        Wou'd

Wou'd you the Portrait of the Fair furvey,
View her in *Terence, Shakefpeare, Fielding, Gay*;
Graceful in Smiles fhe evermore appears,
Nor Earth-born Gnomes with Critic Goofe-
           quills fears.

Falfe Delicacy points the opiate Way,
Where fickly *Affectation* bears the Sway;
True Delicacy points th' enliv'ning Road,
Where *Virtue, Truth,* and *Nature* make Abode.

The LAMENTATION of a MOUSE in a TRAP.

I.

" UNhappy Maid! within this wiry Cave,
 Death's certain Summons doom'd, alas,
  to wait!
Shall curft *Grimalkin's* Guts prove *Muzzy's* Grave?
So young!—In Pleafure's Spring to meet my
  Fate?

II.

Thofe Jet-bead Eyes, that fir'd Beholders' Hearts,
 This Velvet Skin, fmall Ears, and Needle
  Claws!
Thofe Whifkers, (often ftil'd Love's keeneft
  Darts)
 Muft they be crufh'd within a Murderer's Jaws?

III.

Was it for this, with daintieft Morfels fed,
 From the fcoop'd Cheefe, or Bacon's tafte-
  ful Side,
Mamma with Tendernefs her *Muzzy* bred,
 Clafp'd me, and call'd me ftill her *Little Pride?*

T

Oft

IV.

Oft wou'd fhe cry——" My dear, my beft-lov'd
  " Care,
 " Touch not your Prey, 'till well the Place
   you fcan;
" *Grimalkin!*—Of that Monfter, oh beware!—
 " And that more favage Two-legg'd Monfter,
  " *Man.*"

V.

I,—wretched I—unheedful of her Love,
 My Duty's Forfeit now untimely pay;
Be warn'd by me, nor thus rebellious prove,
 Ye Mice!—but ah!—your Parents' Lore obey.

VI.

To poor Papa had this fad Hour been giv'n,
 How wou'd the Sight his tender Bofom wound!
But poor Papa---(fuch the high Will of Heav'n!)
 Laft *April*-day was in a Cream-Bowl drown'd.

VII.

Where now thofe gay coquettifh Breezes?——
  Where?
 That erft fo many youthful Hearts have won?
In Swarms to *Muzzy's* Hole wont to repair,
 And fwear her Beauties far outfhone the Sun.

       They

VIII.

They call'd me Goddefs :——Said, " My Frown
　　" or Smile
　" Cou'd fave or doom to Death the nibbling
　　" Breed ;"
Ye mortal Goddeffes of *Albion*'s Ifle,
　Oh! think——Ev'n Goddefs *Muzzy*'s doom'd
　　to bleed.

IX.

And muft I die ? No more *Squeekero*'s Strain
　(*Squeekero!* lovelieft Youth of youthful Mice!)
Shall flatt'ring Homage pay ;—in Hopes to gain
　That Heart, whofe Worth he fwore was paft
　　all Price.

X.

His lengthen'd Tail !——But, ah, that Tail
　　no more,
　Nor Heroe's Form again fhall blefs my Sight;
His Wit, which fet the Table on a Roar,
　Poor *Muzzy*'s Soul fhall ne'er again delight.

XI.

How oft, *Squeekero,* have you vow'd—" No Pow'r
　On Earth, from your Embrace fhou'd *Muzzy* tear;"
Let not *Grimalkin*'s fpiked Jaws devour,
　But from this horrid Cave your *Muzzy* bear.

Methinks

XII.

Methinks the fell Devourer I espy,
  With Eyes like fiery Suns that flash forth
            Dread;
And Tail like threat'ning Comet rais'd on high,
  And Giant Paw, prepar'd to strike me dead.

XIII.

No Parent, Lover, Friend, at that sad Hour,
  On Lightning's Wings to fly with vengeful Aid!
And can ye—Can ye let the Fiend devour
  Ah me!—Your Darling—your poor *little Maid?*

XIV.

Squeekero! Parents! Friends!—like Lightning fly,
  Bring Armies —— quick —— tear, rend this
            hated Jail:
No Parent, Lover, Friend—alas is nigh——
  Nor cou'd whole Armies in this Cafe avail.

XV.

Ah no! *Squeekero!* Parents! Come not near,
  Left your fond Heart should break to fee
      me thus:
To your wife Precepts had I lent an Ear,
  Poor *Muzzy* had not fall'n a Prey to Pufs.

                                        The

XVI.

The Bait, which but a few fhort Minutes paft,
  So tempting,—now how hateful to mine Eyes!
Repentance oft attends a liquorifh Tafte;
    From *Muzzy*'s Fate learn, Maidens, to be wife.

XVII.

A certain Judgment (fuch Heav'n's wife Decree)
  Attends the Wretch who not a Parent hears;
But hark—the dreadful Latch is rais'd—and fee—
    Have Mercy, Heav'n!—a Two-legg'd Fiend
      appears."

XVIII.

She faid——and, trembling, fweeps the Wires;—
    when, lo!
Murd'rous *Grimalkin*, darting baleful Fires,
Enters the Room:——*All Nature feels the Blow*;
    Poor *Muzzy* fqueeks,—and with a Nip expires.

An EPILOGUE.

Spoken by Mrs. P. in the Character of HYPOLITA,
in She Wou'd or Wou'd Not.

THERE'S Something furely in this Drefs
    infpires,
And with unufual Glee and Courage fires;
For thus accout'red—Damme—Who's afraid
Of bluft'ring Blood or Buck, or ev'n Cockade?
For a cool Thruft if any are inclin'd,
Let 'em approach—in me their Man they'll find:
Their Man, I fay—More Title I can fhow
To *Man*—than many a puny, trifling Beau.

Were it a Rule—a Rule by all agreed,
That none fhou'd pafs for Men, but Men indeed,
How, mighty Sirs, would your large Numbers
    dwindle,
And Swords be chang'd to Diftaff and to Spindle.

At public Places with my Opera Glafs,
I cou'd fhine out a Buck of the Firft Clafs:
" A fine Piece that, my Lord—a damn'd fine Face;
" She's quite the Thing----*Bon Soir*----A Girl's
    the Cafe:
                                        " A

" A Bagnio and a Supper:—She's my own:——
" She has me in her Eye—*Tres humb.*—I'm gone."

[Sings, *Love and Wine give ye Gods, or take back, &c.*]

Suppose, in Time of War, a Female Band
Shou'd, for the Honour of their Native Land,
In Regimental Uniforms appear,
(Come, come, good Sirs, you need not laugh
　　　　　and sneer)
A *British Amazonian Band*, if led
By Major General *P*----- at their Head,
Not *Prussia*'s King, the Heroe of the Age,
With Us, brave as he is, wou'd dare engage.

And at Reviews, there we shou'd doubly shine;
When drest and powder'd we shou'd look divine:
How graceful to the Fife shou'd we advance!
Keep Time—and Step by Step—half march—
　　　　　half dance:

[*Hums a Minuet Tune, and takes 'em off in their Marching.*]

We'd charge, prime, cock, discharge, recharge—
　　　　　then shoulder;
And like Militia Men look bold—nay bolder:
Now to the Right—Now to the Left—and then—
We're quicker in our Motions far—than Men.

If, my good Female Friends, with me you'll
　　　　　join,
And a Petition to this Purpose sign;

　　　　　　　　　　　　The

The Parliament now fits;——in *Y--* fair City,
We could of Heroines—tho' Brave yet Pretty,
A Regiment raife: Perhaps, as a Reward,
The King may chufe Us for his Body Guard;
And if he fhou'd—(may Heav'n's beft Love at-
      tend him!)
We'd proudly lay our Lives down to defend him.

An

An E P I L O G U E.

By A R A M I N T A, *in the* Confederacy.

OUR Poet, tho' for Wit and Humour fam'd,
   For Want of Moral has been fometimes
      blam'd;
Unjuftly fure: The Charaƈters he paints,
I own, refemble Sinners more than Saints:
But Sinners fhou'd be brought upon the Stage,
(For fuch there are, ev'n in this *Bleffed* Age)
Or how fhou'd We, fo Virtuous and fo Good,
Learn to avoid the Snares of Flefh and Blood:
Vice here expos'd, as Vice, is fully fhown;
Old *Nick,* by his Club-Foot is always known.

   Ye naughty Hufbands, and ye naughty Wives,
From what ye've feen, learn to amend your Lives;
But chief, ye *Gripes* and *Moneytraps,*—for You
Our Moral Bard his Moral Leffon drew:
Be *Generous;* nor abroad for Pleafure roam,
Hunt not for Game which you may ftart at Home:
Confider,—Wives forfaken can with Eafe
Repay you---Tit for Tat---whene'er they pleafe;
While you intrigue Abroad, devoid of Grace,
A *Cicefbey* may fill your vacant Place:
For loving Wives take it extremely ill,
When Hufbands fmuggle Grift to a ftrange Mill.

                   When

When in the Matrimonial Knot we're bound,
The Obligation Mutual fhould be found ;
For *Bills of Rights* our Lordly Mates contend,
We too have *Rights* and *Charters* to defend ;
On flow *Petitions* They their Hopes may build,
We'll boldly dare *our* Rulers to the Field ;
Where Face to Face, fhou'd they our Prowefs try,
Poor Souls! we'd cool their Courage prefently.
Let us at leaft an equal Pow'r maintain,
And like King *Will* and *Mary* jointly reign.

Ye mighty Sirs, who aim at fov'reign Sway,
And think poor Wives are born but to obey,
If you wou'd have us true to Honour's Race,
Be you our Guides---we'll follow in the Chace:
Adhere yourfelves to this fame *wond'rous* Plan,
We promife to be good----*as e'er we can.*

The CONTEST.
A VISION.

LAST Night, as mufing on my Bed I lay,
  And Mimic Fancy rul'd with boundlefs Sway,
Sleep gently lull'd my Faculties to Reſt,
And Fairy *Mab* with Magic charm'd my Breaſt;
Methought I ſtood near *Helicon*'s fam'd Stream---
(Critics, obferve---all this was but a Dream:)
Where *Tragedy*, with ſlow and ſtately Pace,
And keen-ey'd *Comedy*, with ſmiling Grace,
Two Siſter Mufes——ſeem'd in warm Debate,
Who beſt deferv'd Pre-eminence of State.

 " With *Jove*'s own Bird the ſhort-wing'd
   " Wren might vie,
" And perch on Heav'n's high Palace in the Sky
" (Exclaims *Melpomene*) as You with Me
" Conteſt prefume in Rank and Dignity :
" Courts, Heroes, Kings----my Verfe fublime
   " require,
" You diſtant gaze---nor dare fo high afpire :
" Ev'n in the inmoſt Chambers of the Soul,
" The fierceſt Paffions own my vaſt Controul;
" While you in lightfome Strains, with tickling
   " Smart,
" Play round the Head, but feldom touch the
   " Heart:
       " In

" In a fuperior Orbit, lo! I fhine ;---

" Think not, vain Girl, your Merit equals mine."

" Cloud-hawling Sifter, quit your high Abode,

" And, if you can, defcend to Reafon's Road,"

(Cries *Comedy*, and curtfey'd as fhe fpoke)

" My Laughter, not my Anger you provoke:

" Our Stations Father *Jove* fix'd here below,

" In Virtue's Caufe to combat ev'ry Foe;

" Our Mirrors to erect, and teach Mankind

" Self-Knowledge in the Portrait of the Mind;

" Vice to unmafk, and Folly to expofe,

" And fhew them, as from Hell they naked rofe:

" Your Province, *Vice*----Mine, *Folly*;----our

　　　　　Succefs

" The different Afpects of our Foes confefs:

" Courts, you avow, is your peculiar Sphere——

" What mighty Wonders has your Glafs wrought

　　　　　" there ?

" Are Kings and penfion'd Courtiers more inclin'd

" To Virtue, than the reft of Humankind ?

" Ah, Sifter! if Mankind I juftly read,

" Courts are unfriendly Soils for Virtue's Seed---

" Ev'n·there—when Rainbow-*Folly* meets your

　　　　　" Eyes,

" Abafh'd, the Coward veils in *Wifdom*'s Guife;

" While bare-fac'd *Vice* with Frontlet glares

　　　　　" of Brafs,

" Nor blufhes at her Portrait in the Glafs.

　　　　　　　　　　" 'Tis

" 'Tis mine, with this keen Lash of Ridicule,
" Tickling to probe each Folly-govern'd Fool;
" To no one Sphere confin'd, I hunt my Game,
" Or Country, City, Court---to me the same:
" Equal with you, through the blue vaulted Sky
" On founding Pinions at my Will I fly;*
" Yet never soar so high, to Reason true,
" But Land-mark Nature still I keep in View:
" Your vain Pre-eminence, sweet Girl, resign,
" If any---that Pre-eminence is mine."

All this sly *Opera* heard, and with a Trill
Which *Echo* answer'd from *Parnassus* Hill,
Her Claim preferr'd:---" In vain your Pow'rs
          " ye boast;
" Know, Sisters, that 'tis *Opera* rules the Roast:
" Mortals by Me possest, now laugh, now cry,
" Expire, revive,---and all---they know not why:
" On Music's Wings *my* Votaries are caught
" To Heav'n, freed from the galling Chain of
          " Thought.
" That Music's Charms can sooth the Savage
          " Beast,
" Among your favourite *Britons* stands confest;
" Let your own Fanes, *Drury* and *Covent* tell,
" Whether or You or *Opera* bears the Bell:
                    U   " The

* *Interdum Vocem tollit Comædia.*

" The Mountain-nurtur'd *Swifs*, whofe callous
    " Souls,
" Not all your *Pathos* or your *Wit* controuls,
" To Me fubmiffive humbleft Homage pay,
" And live or die obedient to my Sway;*
" And what my Influence proves beyond Compare
" *Caftratos* now are Favourites of the Fair."

Melpomene, with Looks of cold Difdain,
(Looks, which ev'n more than Words her Thought
    explain)
Juft glanc'd Contempt, nor deign'd to make Reply
When thus, with Mirth replete, brifk *Comedy*
Retorts :---" Thou mere Vacuity ! Thou Thing
    " of Air !
" In Merit fhall *Sol fa* with us compare !
" Hence, and thy Diftance know, and thank
    " kind Heav'n,
" If in our Train an humble Lot is giv'n :
" At beft, the outward Flourifh you difpenfe
" To deck and ornament Dramatic Senfe;

         " Shall

---

* As a ftriking Inftance of the Power of Mufic, the *Swifs*,
who are not a People of the quickeft Senfation, are faid to
have at this Time a Tune, which, when played upon their
Fifes, infpires them with fuch a Defire of revifiting their native Country, that if prevented, they languifh and die of
Grief. This Tune is therefore, under fevere Penalties, forbid to be played by the *Swifs* Regiments in foreign Service,
as it wou'd infallibly caufe them to defert.

" Shall Truth and Nature, like a frothy Beau,
" Fix all their Merit in vain empty Show?"——

 More she had said, but *Phœbus* from his Throne,
Thus ftopp'd Debate, and *Jove's* high Will
   made known.;
" Sifters, for Shame! (he cry'd)-----Your Strife
   " forbear,
" Mufe againft Mufe is moft unnatural War;*
" To moralize and polifh Humankind,
" Is the great Tafk by Parent *Jove* affign'd;
" Your Mirrors to erect to human Eyes,
" And make Mankind more happy, good, and wife.

 " To combat Giant *Vice*, to mend the Heart,
" To draw forth *Virtue's* Tears---and Joys impart,
" Which none but Good and Feeling Souls
   " can know,
" Be Yours, *Melpomene* :---While Folly's Foe
" *Thalia* ftands confeft; and Heart and Head
" Frees from thofe Weeds, too apt to overfpread
" The Human Soil : Oft-times the richeft Ground
" Will, if neglected, moft in Weeds abound :
" Large and extenfive either Scenic Field,
" Equal the mutual Benefits they yield;
" Equal be then your Rank :----'Tis *Jove's*
   " Decree,
" Henceforth ye live in kindred Amity,
" Nor either claim unjuft Precedency.

   U 2   " By

---

* Dunce againft Dunce is moft unnatural War.   POPE.

" By *Senſe prepar'd* to raiſe the Soul on high
" To Heav'n, upon the Wings of Harmony,
" *Opera*, that Taſk be Yours: But, *Unprepar'd*
" By Senſe, in vain'the Strain deluſive's heard :
" Your Province is to ſee your pleaſing Aid,
" Dependent, at your Siſters' Call diſplay'd :
" Aided by thee, they ſooner ſhall controul,
" And pour the Balm of Virtue in the Soul;
" But for the *Lead*---to that drop all Pretence,
" *Sound* ſtill muſt yield Precedency to *Senſe:*
" They never in the Vanguard ſhou'd appear,
" Whoſe Station's fix'd by Heaven in the Rear:
" Friends all! Henceforth like Siſters kindly love,
" And Heav'n and Earth the Union will ap-
" prove.----

To *Jove*'s Award the Siſters lowly bow'd,
And cloſe embracing, mutual Friendſhip vow'd;
Link'd like the *Graces* Hand in Hand they ſped,---
The Watchman call'd the Hour :--The Viſion fled.

To C. L O E.. Begging a Reconciliation.

'TWIXT *Siam*'s fam'd Kingdom and *Ava*'s
    Domains,*
When long-banifh'd Peace a Re-union attains,
As Emblem of Love, and Extinction of Hate,
A Hole is dug deep in the Midft of each State;
The Earth ta'en from *Ava*'s rich Soil is trans-
    ferr'd,
And quickly in *Siam*'s deep Bowels interr'd;
While that dug from *Siam* in friendly Return,
Finds honour'd Interment in *Ava*'s dark Urn;
Dear *Cloe*, fweet *Cloe*, let Peace be announc'd,
Your Terms I fubmit to, whatever pronounc'd;
But, oh!——that our Union more lafting may
    prove,
Let's twine on the Olive the Rofes of Love;
Like *Siam* and *Ava* our Friendfhip atteft,
And deeply interr'd in each other, find Reft.

* Two Neighbouring Kingdoms in the *Eaft-Indies*.

On Miſs ------, fanning herſelf.

PANTING with Heat from *Sol*'s unnerving
      Rays,
A Fan unfurl'd the lovely Nymph diſplays;
The flutt'ring Toy awakes the dormant Breeze,
And to her throbbing Breaſt gives cooly Eaſe:
The waving Tucker, Wind-impell'd——(Oh
      Heav'n!
Wou'd to my Lot that Blifs ſupreme were giv'n!)
Playfully wanton, now with Kiſſes greets
Thoſe Lilly-cover'd Hills of breathing Sweets;
Now flowing back, to the charm'd Gazer ſhows
A fairer Heav'n than ev'n *Elyſium* knows;
The heaving Mounds alternate fall and riſe,
Darting bewitching Poiſon to our Eyes;
While *Cupid* laughing, from his ſlopy Vale,
Pours flaming Arrows thick as Storms of Hail;
Above the Battery of her Stays now peeps,
Flackers his Wings,—then downward, neſtling,
      creeps
To purling Streams, and conſecrated Groves,
The hallow'd Birth-place of his Mother's Doves;
Where lies, conceal'd from vulgar Eyes, *Love*'s
      Seat,
His *Sans Souci*, his favourite Retreat.

                       Can

Can that which Coolnefs to the Fair imparts,
Thus raife a Wild-fire in Beholders' Hearts?—
In Mercy, heav'nly Maid, our Pains redrefs,
And kindly *give* us more, or *fhow* us lefs.

To Mr W——, *on his Edition of* Shakefpeare.

WHEN *Shakefpeare's* tow'ring Genius,
　　Up to the Heav'ns wou'd fhoot,
　You pull him from his *Pegafus,*
　　And make him walk on Foot.

PHIL--

THUS my Head to Heart said,
  " Zoons, what is the Matter,
" You jump fo, and thump fo,
  " And make fuch a Clatter?"
" *I'm wounded, confounded,*
  " *And ftruck with a Dart,*
" *From the Eyes of fair* Phillis,"
Replies my poor Heart.

II.

" No, Wonder you thunder,
  " And fwell fo with Grief;
" If you're wife, fhun thole Eyes,
  " And feek elfewhere Relief."
" *Poh, a F—t,*" cries my Heart,
  " *My Flame I'll ne'er fmother;*
" *From her, I'd prefer*
  " *Death, to Life with another.*

III.

" *So witty, fo pretty,*
  " *Her Senfe fo refin'd;*
" *Her Mein, like* Jove's *Queen,*
  " *And fuch Goodnefs of Mind;*

                                 " *On.*

" *On her Breaſt, that ſoft Neſt,*
" *Wou'd to Heav'n 'twere my Home;*
" *Doubly bleſt, there I'd reſt,*
" *Nor henceforward wou'd roam.*"

IV.

So ſaid, away fled
   My poor Heart in Deſpair,
And ſighing, kept trying
   To ſoften the Fair:
She bouncing, and flouncing,
   Show'd nought but Diſdain;
While ſhiv'ring, broke and quiv'ring,
   My poor Heart was ſlain.

V.

At moſt, like a Ghoſt,
   Now I wander about,
While *Phillis*, her Will is,
   To jeer, ſneer, and flout:
Tho' I talk, eat, and walk,
   And on Roaſt Beef regale;
Tho' I laugh, ſing and quaff——
   Yet I'm dead as Door Nail.

On

On reading some E A S T E R N T A L E S,
lately publifhed.

THESE *Eaftern* Tales, fo *prettily* expreft,
(Effufions from the Goofe-quills of the *Weft*)
Thofe frigid Nothings fpeak their Mud-fprung
    Birth,
Their Parents Mole-ey'd Gnomes, incor'd with
    Earth;
While *Hawkfworth*'s Eagle Genius foars on high,
Wings to the *Eaftern* Chambers of the Sky;
There the enraptur'd Bard the God infpires,
And with his *Oriental* Magic fires;
His Pow'r Sprites, Demons, Genii, all confefs;—
He paints---and *Fancy* wears her richeft Drefs:---
The *Talifman* his Pen, that charms at Will,
Not *Salomon* cou'd ufe it with more Skill:
Invention glows---while Virtue guides each Line;
We read---we feel the Magic all Divine.——
Ye paltry Scriblers hide your feeble Rays,
Hawkfworth alone can pour the *Eaftern* Blaze.

The

The CONNOISSEUR.*

IN that fam'd Room where Artifts. ftrive,
True Tafte and Genius to revive,†
Where Modern *Guidos* put in Claim,
Contending for the Wreath of Fame;
Where *Virtù*'s Sons with great Precifion
Their Knowledge prove by wife Decifion;
A Judge allow'd, a *Connoiffeur*,
With Buckram Gait, and Phiz demure,
Noting a Piece, on which the Crowd
Unufual Compliments beftow'd,
His Glafs firft peeps thro' with an Air,
(True *Connoiffeurs* fhort-fighted are)
The Painting carelefly furvey'd,
And when inform'd 'twas *Englifh* made,
Thus to an Elbow-Friend, with Look
Oracularly Cynic, fpoke :——
" Sure never was Performance feen,
" More Gothic, taftelefs, lifelefs, mean:
" Painting !—'Tis Canvafs fpoil'd!—Oh, Gad !
" 'Tis daubing !—Execrable !—Sad !

" No

* The Thought on which this Fable is founded, was taken
from the ingenious Mr *Stevens*'s Lecture on Heads.

† The Exhibition-Room in the *Strand*.

" No Colouring! Keeping!—And fuch *Clare-*
" *Obfcure!*—All *Englife!*—All *Barbare!*
" And how unnaturally fhows
" That ill-made Fly on the vile Rofe!
" A Fly! 'tis no more like"—When quick,
Pointing toward the Fly his Stick,
To prove his Criticifm true,
Away the little Infect flew.

F I N I S.

www.ingramcontent.com/pod-product-compliance
Lightning Source LLC
Chambersburg PA
CBHW030804020726
47499CB00006B/1764